SAM BASS

MEETS

THE

MOUNTAIN

MAN

A WESTERN ADVENTURE

DAVID WATTS

FOREWORD FROM ROBERT HANLON

It is with great pleasure that I present to you— yes you! Our wonderful readers—a brand new Western entitled "Sam Bass Meets The Mountain Man." This new frontier Western action novel is just the kind-of thing I have been noticing readers becoming interested in lately. I hope you enjoy this story as much as I did. David Watts has taken a historical character and has placed him in an action-packed story. You'll enjoy it.

- Robert Hanlon – Bestselling author of the "Timber" series, and many other Western adventures.

Wait...

Have you tried this recent Western adventure from David Watts?

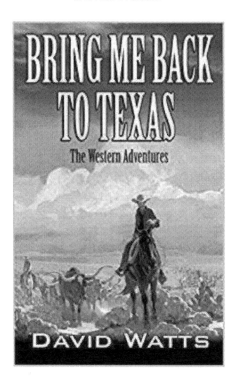

Search for this book on Amazon to add it to your collection...

CHAPTER ONE

I'm Sam Bass. Maybe you've heard the name.

I didn't set out to get famous. I was just having my kicks. Well maybe, it was friction. Friction between need and opportunity. You know. You probably know about that.

What I mean is, the need was being hungry. Opportunity was a gold shipment on its way from San Francisco to New York riding on a train. Too much, *way* too much heat, to walk away from.

I'd just driven a bunch of cattle from San Antonio to Wyoming and spent all the money I got from that on whiskey and women—that will tell you right there that robbing was my long suit and responsibility, my short. Maybe I'll tell you a little secret right now while I'm thinking about it.

Women *love* bad men. You might not believe it, but it's true. I didn't think they would, neither. I mean, these are the men they can't possibly hope to make good again but somehow, some way, they like to *think* they can. Maybe it's the excitement. I guess they are suckers for a little wahoo in their boring lives.

Okay. So when we robbed that train everybody knew about it from Texas to Montana and back again, from San Francisco to New York City, spreading like wildfire. Every time I'd walk into a bar the guys would buy me beer and the women. . . well, you know the rest. More women than I could shake a stick at. And I'm not the prettiest buckaroo on the prairie, neither.

If you know my name, you also know by now that I, with five other saddle-squatters, did, in fact, rob that train. Cleaned it plum out of its precious cargo.

1

Created a huge hullabaloo, that did. They chased us right out of Nebraska and the six of us split two-by-two in all directions like some kind of bomb exploding. Some went to Canada, some got shot, some (me) got away to Texas. On the way my buddy and I ran into a posse so I had to play like I was hunting those train robbers myself and join up with that god forsaken bunch of losers for a while, that verysame posse that was looking for me and had nothing but death shining out of its eyes. You see, they didn't know what the robbers looked like so we passed for joiners. After a few nights I slipped out and hightailed it off to Texas.

Had to lay low a while back home. Let the dust settle. Let memory grow fuzzy, you know, forgetful. I knew Texas like my tabletop. Hid the gold where nobody could find it. Ever. Drove wagons for a while and became acquainted all over again with all the roads, the back-roads, the trails through the thicket, the mountain passes, and caves. Great for hiding, for giving your pursuit the slip.

Truth is, I made the proud and famous Texas Rangers look like wimpy five year-olds. Why, when I got going again I'd rob a bank, fire a few shots in the air and take off. The Rangers would come riding up a storm, mad as hell, and I'd just disappear like a mirage out on the high Texas Prairie. Pissed off those Rangers something awful. Tarnished their stupid, big fat egos, is what it did.

The Rangers got serious and started asking around looking for the people who took me in and hid me from time to time and things got a little too hot to handle.

You might wonder why anybody would take in a wanted criminal, a bank robber, a stealer of gold on a train to New York, a consort with their women. I'll tell you a secret. A lot of people would. What I discovered by accident is most people would *love* to be that person who rides alongside a train on his lightning fast horse, swings onto the car at breakneck speed, pushes the guards aside like they were broom straws, blows open the safe and steals the gold. That's what I learned. People always wanting to hear how I did it as if listening to the story made them feel like they were part of it.

And I'll tell you another thing. Nobody likes bankers. How could they? All they do is make it hard for you to get a loan to buy your house or your farm, then interest you so hard so that when you have trouble keeping up with the payments they can come along and take away your property and all the money you already paid for it. It's legalized robbery, ain't it? People love to see that kind of person smacked down. And, secretly, they love the one who has the balls to do it.

Maybe you know, the Texas Rangers don't care about that "banker" kind of thievery. You never see them going after bankers. Those are the folks that pay their salary. And since I was making the Rangers look so bad the politicians got in on it and turned the screws. Everything escalated after that. That became what they called the "Bass War." Made me proud to have my name on a war but that sense of pride lasted about ten seconds. Next thing I know they're hot on my tail shooting live ammo and I had to git.

That's when I disbanded the gang, for a while, and took off to the mountains not super far beyond the New Mexico border.

Now some people might say this part of a history, this story I'm going to talk about never happened.

That's because it ain't in any history books. There are no newspaper articles about it, neither. It's not even in the folklore that gets passed generation to generation. That's because... *nobody was there.*

Down around the Rio Grand there's lots of mountains most people don't even know about. Lots of canyons to ride through, caves and overhangs to hide in. It's an outlaw's paradise. And it's so far away from everything that people forget you exist. I tried that out for a while but it didn't suit my temperament.

I kept going until I got that sweet smell of pine needles rising to my nose from the forest floor. Now that was a little slice of heaven. I figured I could stay here for a while. Trouble is, you have to get there to stay there.

There were times I regretted my decision to go way out there. I knew the Blackland Prairie. I knew the Hill Country. I knew the Piney Woods of East Texas, the panhandle plains, the lakes and rivers and where the quicksand could suck you down to bedrock. I even knew the Lost Pines down around Bastrop and how to get through them Loblolly critters without having a clear path to see through. But out west, up the escarpment to the Edwards Plateau, it was wide open and flat as a griddlecake. That means they can see you sharp as a jaybird from a country mile away and follow your trail like chalk on a blackboard.

I had to keep my distance. No fires at night. No standing for long periods on hills and promontories where I could be seen. Hiding behind boulders and trees wherever I could find them. Riding up the middle of streams as far as I could. And choosing terrain to travel on that doesn't very easy take horse prints.

Out around Abilene country they just about caught up with me. To my left was a butte flat as a table on top, pocked here and there with low shrubbery. There was a spur of that butte off in front of me, sliding down in height little by little until it was almost low to the ground. I kicked Speed Boy, my paint, into a gallop and looped around the low end of the spur, followed along behind it in some tall grass where I couldn't be seen and rode up a small canyon all the way to the top. I situated myself behind a large rock and watched below as the Rangers hunted for prints among the tall grass. I knew it would take them a long time to pick up the trail so I pushed on, tracking along a somewhat different path to the west.

This would be a test for the Rangers. How bad did they want to keep after me? They would know they'd lost that short distance they'd covered between us. And the terrain was getting rougher, more desolate. As far as I knew there was no bounty on my head so they might not have enough reason to keep them from missing their firesides and their wives and pull back home. Especially since there were still tribes of Comanche and Apache out around here.

I rode a little longer that day, stopping only for grazing where I found it and here and there for a little water from a stream or small pond. Night found me in the open prairie and I pushed as far as I could into the half-moon evening but had to stop to rest both horse and rider in the middle of gawd almighty nowhere. I stood down from my horse and looked around. It seemed to me that we were the tallest structures out here, casting ironic looking moonshadows on the ground.

No shelter. No place to hide. Unfamiliar territory. Hostiles everywhere.

I made camp, such as it was, chewed on a little jerky, hobbled my horse and put the saddle on the ground as a pillow for my head.

I slept uneasy. I dreamed of a girl named Blossom and how sad it was I couldn't settle down. But then the dreams turned to gunfights in the streets of San Saba, me against the whole goddamned town. I fought off the dreams but strange sounds woke me in the middle of the night. The half moon was setting in the west so that meant it was close to midnight. There was just enough light to catch the silhouettes of three Indians circling my small camp. They came up to my camp, drew their bowstrings and filled my bedroll with arrows. That's when I came around from behind the rock, drew my pistol and shot two of them. An arrow grazed my shoulder. I shot in the direction it came from but I only heard the sound of a horse galloping swiftly away.

I slept uneasy, got up early, left for parts west, leaving my bedroll stuck to the ground with three arrows still in it. Some kind of monument, I suppose, a message for whoever happened upon it before it dissolved into the turf. Didn't want to sleep in that cursed thing ever again.

I'd been chased pretty bad. You make those Texas Rangers pissing mad and suddenly they remember how to come after a man. They drive at you like they're the Union Army on a Biblical Crusade. It's an awful thing having to deal with men who think that God is on their side.

They came at me with both barrels a-firing, yelling like a mess of Apaches on a warpath. I'm fast, and I'm smart, and I know the territory, but I'm just one man and they were five.

Then there's these unpredictable, wild-ass Indians. Sometimes they are the enemy and sometimes the savior. Most people don't know that I spent a little time with the Comanche. What they know about being impossible to catch would fill a book as thick as the Old Testament. I can't do what they do but I did learn how to double back on my trail to fool my followers. And how important it was to skip the idea of building a fire at night so as not to give them anything to point their compass at.

Between my stealth and a little Comanche foxiness I'd managed to survive this chase long enough but I was running out of supplies and water was getting scarce.

What I did was to travel by night when it was cooler and my horse and I needed less water. The moon was moving from half to full so that helped. Then I hid out during the day and slept. Using this trick I managed to make it a little ways up into the Rocky Mountains with nobody in sight.

And there, it was, that I collapsed. My horse wandered away but I was way too spent to chase after it.

David Watts

CHAPTER TWO

I slept for a day and a half. Least I think that's what I did. I woke to the sting of my parched, blazing skin and the same feeling on my tongue. I made an effort to rise but could not, so I rolled on one side. As I did so, an amazing sight came to my blurry eyes. There beside me was a military canteen and a bundle wrapped up in the cured skin of a rabbit. I gobbled water from the canteen and resisted my very strong urge to quickly gobble more, remembering the sad tragedies of over anxious, dehydrated men.

As the water rose in my body I had enough strength to untie the bundle and see what was inside. There, lined up in a neat row, were three sticks of jerky, from what animal I could not begin to tell. But I have to say, it didn't fucking matter to me where they came from for I scarfed them down in one monster hurry.

My stomach ceased growling. My muscles found some life and I rose to a sitting position. And then I made an astonishing discovery. My horse was tied to a tree and at its feet was a bowl of water and a pile of hay.

I struggled to stand but fell back to a sitting position. I rested and massaged my mistreated muscles back to a few sparks of life. They resisted my efforts but finally recovered enough strength to stand erect and take a deep breath.

With great effort I mounted my horse with my rubbery legs dangling to the side and rode to the peak of the promontory just ahead. I regret to admit I had no memory for the moments that lead up to my loss of consciousness. Just as well. No time to spend on remorse.

At the top of the overlook I could see down a long valley. The sun was peaking over the horizon in the east and it cast a resonant glow through the haze and mist rising off the prairie. My eyes slowly grew accustomed to the brilliance and began to make out rocks and trees and streams and a long, long desert-like stretch of land that seemed to be deserted by every living thing.

Mainly, I saw no evidence that Texas Rangers had extended their search into the region. That's what I was looking for.

Reassured, that at least for the moment, I was safe, I set about finding some way of survival. The season was autumn, which in these territories allowed sufficient warmth for gathering foods, preparing shelter, and generally getting ready for the coming winter. I decided I'd hunt for my dinner but at the end of the day I had but one measly squirrel. I went to sleep hungry and still weak as a push of that whiff of tiny breeze that trails off a passing wagon.

Next morning same. Hay and water and canteen and jerky. If I was tempted to think that in my semi-delusional state the first morning up here in the altitude that the little gifts I'd received were nothing more than an hallucination of mine, I had to think again. I decided to catch whoever it was bringing all this stuff.

I thought I might use the same technique I'd used on my Indian attackers out on the prairie so I stuffed what I had that resembled a bedroll, placed my saddle under the head and hid behind a small thicket.

Nothing happened all night long and I was cursing my luck when I rose to start my day and as I stood up I bumped into something behind me. I turned quickly to see a man standing there. His face was gaunt, his chin was covered with a medium length grey beard and he had piercing eyes that looked straight through a person. His skin was burnt from years out in the sun and his hair was unkempt and dangled to his shoulders like strands of a mop. He wore a Muskrat hat and a buckskin jacket with ribbons of leather dangling from his sleeves. He wore rawhide pants and under his cuffs was a pair of Indian moccasins. He was dressed in such a way it would be hard to distinguish him from an Indian.

"You didn't *really* figure you could catch me, did ya?" he said. "I know every Indian trick in the book and a few more I writ myself. Not been fooled by anyone since I got here and you're not the first to try."

"I'm obliged," I said, "for the victuals."

"Can't let a man starve to death, though you did give it a pretty good try."

"Not my territory," I said.

"Didn't have to tell me that."

He turned and started walking away.

"Wait," I said.

"If you're coming you better get your horse and gear," he said.

He walked and I followed, leading my horse. I noticed how with great skill he put his feet in places where there were no sharp rocks, no sticks to crack, no leaves to rustle. No wonder I didn't hear him coming.

We walked maybe an hour, saying nothing. But I was aware of his vigilance. He spotted a rattlesnake before it could danger us. He watched the gyre of the vultures for signs of rotting carcasses. He seemed to be alert to every moving thing in every corner of his piece of the world.

Directly, we arrived at a small cabin tucked up against a stone cliff with a sizeable overhang shading all but the corner of the front porch. There was a spring nearby surrounded by a patch of green grass and a small garden fenced in with chicken wire. Pelts of rabbit, beaver, fox and deer hung from a line that stretched from his porch to a large oak standing off to the right side.

He stopped and pointed up the valley. "What do you see there?" he said.

"The end of the valley," I said.

"That's what any tenderfoot would see. Look again."

I looked again. What was he wanting me to see? I saw red clay along the floor. There were patches of sage, a few scrub oaks, scattered boulders that must have fallen from the walls surrounding the valley.

"What are we looking for?" I said.

"My back door," he said.

I looked again. At the end of the valley the right wall of the surrounding cliffs seemed to veer slightly inward as it approached the end. Then it curved back to a dead end. Since he was suggesting escape I took a risk and made up something to describe what I couldn't exactly see. "There's a chink in the wall off to the right," I said, "that connects through to the next valley. My guess is that's your hidden passage to freedom in case of attack."

My guide cocked his head to one side and nodded just slightly. "You might be easy to train," he said and went inside.

CHAPTER THREE

"Who're ya running from?"

The inside of his house was remarkably well-appointed. There was a black walnut table and chairs, a small desk. There was even a bookcase with several books in it. At a distance I could identify a Bible and a large volume entitled "A history of the World." A daybed against the side wall was covered with bearskin and a fireplace stood against the opposite wall.

"You might be the type to rob banks," he said, "but I reckon you're no murderer." He scowled at me. "Don't look like the murdering kind."

He sat in a rocking chair and motioned me to a small stool. "But somebody's chasing you."

"Just a few Texas Rangers."

He started shaking tobacco into a trough of paper, raised his hand to offer. I refused. "They must want you pretty bad cause they never come out this far."

"They got their dander up for not being able to catch me back home."

He eyed me with suspicion. "You'd have to be pretty slick. They're a bunch of crazy jackasses most of the time, but they can locate a scorpion in a wood pile when they want to. I gather they couldn't find you."

"I know my territories."

He nodded. "But not this one," he said, and pointed at me with his wet, droopy cigarette.

I waited for him to go on.

He lit the soggy thing. "When you got here you camped right near an Apache settlement. I figure they must be in a pretty good mood or you'd be food for dogs by now."

I told him about my encounter with three Indians out on the prairie.

"That would be Comanche," he said. "A renegade band of ruffians. They're like vultures 'cause they thrive on travelers passing through. They must have thought you'd not be smart enough to trick them at their own game." He laughed. "The old bedroll trick!" he said. He shook his head. "You're damn lucky to be alive."

"I reckon so. But you helped a bit, lately."

He just grunted in response. He rocked back and forth. "Anyway. Time to check my traps. You comin'?"

"Nothin' on my schedule."

And we took off, but not before he made a poultice out of some foul smelling leaves for my shoulder and fed me the kind of grub you'd expect from a mountain man: some kind of unrecognizable porridge that tasted like swamp mixings, a blackened piece of flat bread and, of course, some jerky. You're wondering from what animal? Don't look at me 'cause I didn't ask.

***

We didn't take his back door exit. We went straight out the valley to his trapping place on a tributary of the Pecos. We talked along the way. I learned that this was Apache territory but there were scattered settlements of Jumano here and there, spilling over from the Pueblo of northern New

Mexico. The latter were more friendly, predictable. Here tell, he had a couple of wives among the Jumano.

I learned his name. Bill Crutchton. He was born in Kentucky, got into a altercation with the local politicians over his right to keep a menagerie of animals in his back yard, decided to move somewhere where there was no government to interfere with his wont to live however way he decided to. Ended up way-the-hell out here.

He traded his pelts with the Indians and with the soldiers at a frontier outpost over at Taos, or once a year as far away as Ben Leaton's Trading post along the Rio Grande. In trade, he got ammunition, sugar, flour, candles, kerosene and assorted essentials. From the Indians he got clothing, large animal furs, and various herbs and medicaments. What he told me about trade was that you had to be honorable. Cheat someone once and your trading days were over.

We traveled horseback. What I noticed was his watchful eye, always scanning the horizon, occasionally turning back to look behind. I felt as if he measured every object and motion in the giant globe of territory that surrounded us.

We arrived at the tributary. He went to his traps and showed me how they worked. He used what he called "Drowning Traps" to catch his prey then drop underwater to drown the beaver or muskrat. Since beaver are very territorial, next to the trap Bill drove a post in the river bottom sticking above the water about 14 inches and rubbed on the top end of the post some oil from the caster gland of another beaver that carries the scent that they use to mark their territory. The local beaver will smell the oil, think a competitor is in the region, become aggressively curious, come to investigate and step in the trap. We pulled up the traps and emptied them of three, very large, beaver. He affixed them to his belt and we turned back to camp.

On the way back we had to ride through a narrow chink in a wall of rock that allowed us through. Half way into the trench he stopped abruptly and sniffed the air.

"Comanche," he said, "and turned his horse around. It was too late. They came at us from both sides and closed off our escape. They had rifles already drawn so there was no time to do battle. Our only hope to stay alive was somehow to endure what comes next.

We found out real soon.

CHAPTER FOUR

The Comanche took us to a clearing surrounded by a few hillocks and beyond them, the mountains. We were contained in what appeared to be a space shaped like an arena for some kind or ceremony or perhaps games of some sort.

They stripped us of our clothing, took our horses, our weapons and made us lie naked out in the sun until our skin baked like cornpone in the skillet. We were surrounded by about twenty Indians, some middle-aged, mostly young braves.

Late in the day the leader came and untied us and took us to the edge of the circle. He pointed in the direction of the far mountain. Behind us he lined up six young braves.

The mountain man turned to me and said, "This is where you just have to forget about any pain you get in your feet and keep running like hell. If they catch us they will tear us apart."

The leader stepped back, drew a pistol and fired two shots just behind our heels. We took off like startled antelope.

Between breaths, the mountain man said, "Don't turn around and don't slow down for anything. If they catch us we'll be food for the vultures."

We ran like there was no tomorrow. My feet bled like stabbed hogs, the pain was unimaginable but, remembering what Bill said, I favored them none. Better to have shredded feet than a shredded body.

Maybe ten minutes into our run we heard two more shots, followed by a lot of whooping and hollering. We knew that our death was riding on the speed and endurance of six very young and pumped up braves.

If we thought we couldn't run any faster we fooled ourselves. My feet had gone beyond pain to numb—almost numb, that is. I felt like I was running on puffs of smoke, only with some fire left inside.

The sounds of our pursuers grew closer. I thought this must be what the doe feels chased by a pack of wolves. In my haste, I tripped on a branch, my tired legs too weak to lift high enough. Bill stopped. We looked back to see one isolated brave, obviously the fastest of the bunch, way out front of the rest. Bill picked up a medium sized stone and stood facing the oncoming brave, standing still as a redwood.

As the brave approached he lifted the spear he was carrying over his head. I knew that with his speed and his strong arm when he launched it, it would run straight through whoever he hit. I decided my life was over and I resigned to die out here in the middle of goddamned nowhere.

First thing I knew, Bill swung the stone like the toss of a javelin, stiff-armed and swift, and, as it turns out, accurate, for it smashed into the head of the oncoming brave. He folded and slumped to the ground.

Bill turned to me.

"Screw up your spirits," he said, "'cause we got one last chance."

Seeing the remainder of the pack oncoming, wild as a wolf pack, hollering like coyote and getting closer, gave me all I needed to boost my energies and I sprung to my feet and started moving.

Having fallen and stiffened I moved slowly at first. Bill stayed with me and egged me on and soon I was keeping up. We were getting spent. We had to find some kind of respite soon or we were dead meat.

Between very quick breaths and in little pieces, Bill said, "When. . . we get. . . to that big. . . red rock. . . follow me. . . do what I do. . . and. . . don't. . . DON'T SLOW DOWN!"

He turned sharply around the rock and I followed two paces behind. He must have known the territory for there was a rather deep beaver pond straight ahead.

"Don't hesitate," he said over his shoulder. Whereupon he dove head first into the pond and started swimming to the bottom. I followed, my lungs exploding with fatigue and now the added insult of no air. But I followed, for to turn back was to face certain dismemberment.

I opened my eyes underwater and saw him swim into a hole in the beaver dam. I was struggling to stay underwater for my oxygen lack was causing me to go wonky in the head. Oh well, I thought, it for sure would be more pleasant to die here under water than it would up where the Indians are.

I followed and it grew suddenly dark. Ahead was a glow occupied by Bill's feet kicking. I was about to explode but I lurched one last effort and came up in a cave. A cave made of sticks and mud. An abandoned beaver den.

I was almost unconscious, breathing so fast I could hardly sustain my very life. My heart was jumping out of my chest. So deprived of oxygen I was that I thought I would never catch up and surely die.

Slowly I came to, and slowly my breathing grew less desperate.

Bill whispered. "Now we have to be absolutely quiet, no matter what happens."

We could hear the Indians outside, chattering among themselves. This must be what beavers hear when danger comes, the slap of the water, the dive into their den.

Then I imagined what it must be like for the Indians to chase your prey into a dead end and then have it vanish. I almost chuckled. Serves them right! I thought they might dive into the water to see where we went but they must have thought it was some kind of trick. Or maybe magic.

I heard the branches of the dam creak and felt the vibrations of feet walking. They even walked on the dome on the top of our den. I could hear them over us but the dam held, the roof held, and after a while, they went away.

CHAPTER FIVE

We dozed a while. I couldn't really sleep because my feet kept waking me up.

By now my feet were twice their size and throbbing like drum.

Bill swam outside to check if anyone was still there. No one had stayed behind. He returned with leaves he'd picked alongside the river and plastered them to our feet until there were several layers of thickness, enough to serve as a slipper to walk on. He tied them to our feet with strips of grapevine and we felt the cool, wet, soothing effect of nature's natural elements upon our injuries.

"We have to get going."

"Where?"

He looked sideways. "Not far. Anyway, we can't stay here."

We swam out. Now the great test. Could we walk?

The first step felt like someone hit the sole of my foot with a hatchet. But the next one was only a ball pein hammer. I hobbled and staggered but somehow managed to follow Bill as he took us up over the banks of the beaver pond, up the rise between mountains to the south and down the other side.

After an hour passed we saw smoke and before we made it to its origin, three Indians approached. Bill spoke something to them in their language and they picked us up and carried us, bruised, battered and still naked into the center of their settlement.

I'd never seen such a place. I thought I'd been transported to another world. Carried into an Indian settlement I expected teepees but was greeted by adobe houses, some of them two story with ladders to the second level. The men shaved their heads but for a patch of hair to hold a feather. Some were naked and others wore breechcloths. They were abundantly tattooed, frequently in stripes. Some of the women were also naked. Others wore deerskin ponchos and skirts of cattle skins. A few were wearing crude multicolor shawls made from cotton grown nearby.

There was a small stream near the far side of the settlement that fed a well- organized spread of irrigation ditches they used to grow their crops. There was corn for the bean vines to climb and squash to cover the ground so that weeds did not take over.

"Where are the teepees?" I asked Bill.

"They only use teepees when they travel on long buffalo hunts," he said. "The Cherokee and Apache are the ones that have teepees in their settlements most times.

We were greeted by the Chief and bundled off into an adobe where we were bathed by four young women and then clothed in skins and delicate cloths. We were offered water and fed perch from the stream along with corn patties, heated to a bronze crusty deliciousness. I could not have wished for more.

When they were done they removed our makeshift sandals and brushed our feet with a cool, syrupy liquid that contained beaver oil, said to relieve pain and draw out swelling. Then after attaching an assortment of leaves they wrapped our feet in woven hemp.

I had many questions heavy on my mind but sleep grabbed my first attention.

***

The first thing I noticed when I woke was an array of multi-colored images painted on the inside walls of the adobe. I must have been too disoriented to have seen them before. The second thing was that Bill was already awake. He was getting his hair combed by one of the women.

"We are among the Jumano Indians," he said. "I trade with them regularly. They are, by comparison, very civilized. They're part of that Pueblo tribe that builds adobe houses—you can see that around here—but other divisions of the tribe to the west of here build cliff dwellings. They can defend themselves pretty well but don't have the same kind of aggressiveness as the Apache or the Comanche."

"You must have known we were not far from here."

"Like I said. . ."

". . . you know the territory," I finished for him.

He just nodded.

Another young woman came in.

"She wants to comb you hair," said Bill.

"After what I've been through, that would be divine."

"It'll be divine in any case."

I nodded because she was beautiful. She commenced brushing my hair. Her name was Moonflower.

Bill turned to his girl. "This is Morning Sunshine," he said. "She's one of my wives."

***

Eventually, I got out of Bill that having more than one wife was sometimes permitted in this tribe, especially in cases where a man dies and, out of respect, his brother takes his wife. She is cared for in this manner and is not so lonely. Most of the Jumano, however, were monogamous.

Moonflower visited me three times every day.

Each day she brought leaf baskets she had made and applied them to my feet. With a piece of bone she scraped away pus and dead skin, massaging the tissue back to life.

When, on the seventh night, the infection in my foot spread into my blood and traveled throughout my body, instinctively she came to me and crawled into the space beside me and wrapped her body around mine, collapsing down the shivers and shakes that were exploding inside me like hundreds of bombs. And I felt some essence, some spiritual element of her arriving within me, coming into the realm of my unstill core and calming the raging forces at battle. Then it was, finally, I began to believe I might actually survive.

Later that night as the fever started downward, I started to sweat. Water rushed out of every pore of my body and I began to stink worse than a wood badger. Still, she stayed with me, shielding me with her body and in the morning when sunlight streamed into the room, she took off my clothing and bathed my aching, exhausted body.

The fever disappeared over the next two days.

***

To pass the time Bill would tell tall tales filled with exaggerations and incredible assertions, like the time he turned a buffalo heard around to scatter a group of Indians intent upon scalping him:

"I was being chased by a small group of Kiowa over in Oklahoma," he said, "mad as hornets and intent upon separating me from my scalp 'cause I'd been hunting their territories, when I came across this herd of buffalo. I don't know what possessed me but I decided to ride directly into the middle of the herd. That added, of course, another danger, that of the buffalo turning on me or crushing horse and rider in the middle of their movable mass of flesh."

"I had a bullwhip lashed to my saddle so I took it out and began popping it in the air. The herd began to move forward with me until we got up a fair amount of speed, when, because the Kiowa were catching up, I moved near the middle of the rocking mass of buffalo then near to the front where I became the leader of the stampede."

"As we rode along I spied a huge rock the shape of a very large egg with a big chink out of the front, rising out of the prairie. I moved ahead of the herd and aimed the mass of rumbling buffalo at the rock, shifting to the left hand side just at the last minute. As I passed the rock I turned sharply to the right, behind the stone, and around toward the front, heading back where we came. I slipped inside the big chink in the stone as the herd sped by, headed directly at the Indians. What resulted from that was the scattering of a sizeable group of Kiowa across the prairie and enough time for me to make my escape."

He paused for effect. Then said, "That's how I used a buffalo herd as my best weapon."

I thought it was a pretty tall tale. When challenged, all he would say was that lying was a badge of honor among mountain men and I had to decide how much was real and how much was entertainment. He said, according to him, lies were playful, much more fun than truth. On a later occasion, however, he did say something really interesting. "Lies tell a different kind of truth."

I was puzzled.

"We wouldn't like them if they didn't," he said.

Seeing me still perplexed he went on. "Take that story about the buffalo herd. Where you might quibble with the details, the story does tell the truth about the possibility of survival made better by quick thinking, and also about the nature of the Kiowa to defend their territory."

I nodded.

"What's also true," he said. "is this: if I can tell you a good enough story you'll stop thinking about your miserable condition."

I came to realize that the best storytellers using techniques Bill talked about, could tell tales no one could forget.

***

We stayed in the Jumano Settlement for two weeks, recovering. Slowly we could tolerate just the slightest pressure on our feet. It was almost like learning to walk again, the feet not cooperating.

It would take another week before we could leave the settlement. In the meantime the Chief equipped us with horses (no saddles, of course) clothes enough to manage and two Winchester rifles. "It's a gift," Bill said, "but I'll have to pay them back with gifts of our own over time. When I was in the other world back east, I never minded making a little money, but this is a better system than banks and money, doncha think? Based on honor, not greed."

David Watts

CHAPTER SIX

Time to leave.

Bill and I were half human again and he was worried about the state of his estate, little as it was, tucked away against the side of the cliff.

Yes, I'd been ready to get back since the day I got to Indian camp but that idea was not worth the effort it took to think about it because without the help of these generous folks we'd have been pickled pork. As fate would have it, the closer it came time to leave the more attached I'd become.

One person in particular, it seems.

I watched sadness well up in her eyes as Moonflower anticipated the time we were to go away. I didn't expect that. But I guess taking care of someone stirs up affection even if there's not much reason for it. Indians try not to show emotion. I know that. Be brave and all that stuff. Turns out, it's possible she may have sensed arising within me, a deepening connection to her, and, therefore, allowed herself to let loose her own.

Bill and I didn't talk about leaving. I *couldn't* talk about it with Moonflower. Even so, that she knew it was coming was obvious. It was one of those foregone conclusions, I guess, reinforced by the kind of speechless understanding that comes from living close together for a while. She probably felt it in her bones.

In case I didn't get the message she was getting attached to me, she started staying later and later at night. When you consider that improvement in health usually means *less* time with your nurse, this was not expected.

Then, that last night in camp she stayed until morning. Previously, her presence was all about my painful feet, the infection that was growing in my severed tissues, my fever, my rigors, my descent into the depths of darkness. I needed her. I depended on her. Now this presence was more about the pleasure of each other's company, the opening of intimacy between two sentient beings that sleeping in the same bed could mean. It made me realize I'd been missing something really important.

As we traveled the pathway back to Bill's house I marveled how one could become so attached to someone in spite of differences in race, language, and culture. Why not? Bill set the example. At least he had the advantage of being able to speak to his Indian wife. Could there be the deepest of connections without language? Apparently so. It's not that I was considering staying behind, I wasn't. I was just realizing that already, thirty minutes later, I missed having her around.

The entrance back into Bill's valley seemed different this time. Maybe it's the kind of unfamiliarity that comes from being away for a while, or maybe because I entered this valley under different circumstances when I came through the first time. This time there was a much stronger feeling that the whole valley lay securely hidden, invisible from the outside world.

High stone cliffs rose to meet us as we approached, making our way through the tall grass. The rocks that made up the wall were irregular and edgy, as if some great hand had reached down to bedrock, cracked loose giant pieces, looped its fingers under the edges and lifted plates of hard rock so vertical as to stand like pickets in a fence.

These stone slabs were arranged so that the entrance to the valley was almost invisible unless you happened to stand in just the right place. This was the secret to its anonymity. You had to be up close and looking down the fence line of vertical rocks to see the wedge of space large enough to admit horse and rider and not a lot more.

The house looked the same. Even the same skins hung on the line. The bean garden had reached maturity and was ready for picking. Inside, we had to throw away perishables but except for the subtle evidence of a few mice here and there, everything was untouched.

Exhausted in mind and body we settled in for a long, dreamless nap.

***

When we got up the sun was well into the next day.

Bill was up rustling around, making ready to go check his traps. Without a saddle for our horses we had no billet ring to attach a long gun scabbard so we both wore sidearms instead. What could be wrong with that?

As we rode over the ridge and down in to the trench that was the Pecos tributary we spied a large grizzly stealing catch from the traps.

We dismounted and fired three times. The grizzly reared up on its hind legs and roared like thunder in a cave. We mounted up, ready to run, but the grizzly turned, splashed its way through the water to the far bank where it collapsed and lay on its side. Motionless.

We waited maybe five minutes.

Seeing no sign of life we stripped to our bare skin, took our knives in our teeth ready to harvest a fresh and valuable pelt and started swimming across the river.

Half-way across, one eye on the grizzly popped open.

Shit!

Bill stopped swimming and said, "Oh for Christ's sake!" Whereupon he started swimming for dear life downstream, with the current, figuring, I guess, that this might be the quickest getaway. I turned back to the shore, flailing like mad.

I looked over my shoulder to see the bear turn downstream in rapid pursuit of Bill who was swimming fast but the bear was faster and soon overtook him.

Just before the bear reached Bill he dove underwater and was invisible. The grizzly reared up and looked around. When Bill surfaced he came up right behind the bear. The bear turned and raised his paw but when it hit the water Bill was already under again, swimming for a piece of stream as far as possible from this gargantuan mass of power and rage.

When he surfaced this time, breathless and exhausted, he was right under the mouth of the bear. The bear roared, opened its mouth showing an amazing collection of teeth, and reared back ready to collect lunch.

I don't know if Bill was too terrified with the prospect of an imminent and painful death to hear the three popping sounds that happened just then, or to see the spurt of blood from the head and eyes of the grizzly hovering over him, because the bear fell on top of him right then. I had finally reached the shore, fumbled among our clothing for the first available pistol and shot wildly at the bear. That I hit him at all in my shaky, charged-up state was a miracle. And Bill, now underwater with a bear weighing him down, discovered that he was not in his grasp and could escape to the surface.

After Bill collected his wits and a little oxygen, we hauled the bear to shore. Bill sat down next to the bear. He was trembling. His eyes flashed and darted. His breath was short and quick. We sat for a while during which time I was unsure what was happening and what I should do. The only thing I knew, and I knew it well, was that I could not force this scene. It would go the way it would go.

Maybe five minutes passed without action. I was aware of the contrast between the furious, death filled activity of a few moments past and this haunting stillness. Both of which, filled with their own quality of tension.

Then Bill did a curious thing. He got up and bent over the head of the bear, all wet and bloody, its eyes still possessing that wildness of the moment before, and he reached down and touched the forehead as if blessing it for its misery and its death.

Not a word was said. Nor did words want to be.

I stood and together we gathered our prize.

***

That evening Bill celebrated the extension of his life by cooking up beans he'd started soaking the morning before and some incredible hushpuppies he fashioned out of corn mash, bread crumbs, and bacon grease on a flatiron skillet. He even got out a bottle of rye whiskey he'd traded for over at Fr. Stanton which resulted in Bill getting drunk as a sailor and singing bawdy sea shanties well into the night.

Then we slept like dogs on opium.

CHAPTER SEVEN

The garden needed attention.

We harvested beans, carrots, radishes, winter squash and collard greens. Some of the foods we dried and kept for later, some required substantial feasting right now. Bill'd already stored corn from the summer harvest he got from the Jumano. Now we added strips of bear meat to the jerky drying in racks he'd made portable so he could move them into a shed at night to protect them from raccoons and skunks.

Since bear meat is so gamey, he took some berries and pounded them into thin strips of meat to make what he called Pemmican, dried flakes of meat seasoned with berries.

By now our feet were almost back to normal yet we still chose to still wear Indian moccasins that were much more comfortable and allowed space for the remaining swelling to go down. We added another layer of cloth inside to thicken the padding.

Bill had restored his traps after the grizzly debacle and we were getting a steady stream of beaver and muskrat. The pelts were piling up. Soon it would be time for trading.

We loaded up some of the best in burlap bags and rode off to the Jumano camp. We were greeted like returning heroes. Bill simply gave the pelts to the village chief as gratitude for how they received us broken and helpless and did an amazing job putting us back together.

We stayed three days. Moonflower came to visit me afternoons and again in the evenings but she did not stay overnight. Bill explained to do so now would mean marriage. She was nothing if not gracious. Yet her eyes radiated a bit of sorrow mixed in with the sweetness.

I was neigh on to asking her about marriage but there was something in my heart that felt like uncertainty. Every time I thought about remaining here with a wife I was reminded of my reputation as an outlaw and that sooner or later there would be a Texas Ranger at my door.

On our last evening I asked Bill to translate my quandary to her. She said she didn't mind. I appreciated her answer but I thought that what she said was a little white lie that had at its root a truth which had more to do with her wish to protect me from worry than it said anything about her true feelings.

We left the following morning. There was a hole in my chest.

***

The winter harvest was done. And the river was beginning to be trapped out. Our stores were rich enough to last for months. We settled in but Bill started looking restless.

"Ever thought about revenge on those monsters who made us run for our lives naked?"

"Thought about it."

"How hard did you think about it?"

We were sitting by a fire on a rainy evening. Bill had started the fire with his equipment from his Strike a Light bag: flint, tender, steel. He was smoking his clay pipe filled with a mixture of his precious tobacco mixed with kinnick-kinnick, apparently some kind of leaf from a local plant used to splice out the tobacco for a few more smokes. He'd made coffee from beans he'd scooped from a white cloth bag with "Pen & Company of New Orleans" written on it, ground them up in a grinder and poured steaming water over them from a pot he kept in the edge of the fire. Then he sweetened the hot liquid with a slice from a cone-shaped slab of brown sugar he kept in a cabinet. He put out some Hardtak, a crisp flatbread made from flower and water, for us to munch on. We were pretty comfortable. The last thing on my mind was going out into a gawdawful storm to hunt down a few surly Indians.

"Not very hard," I said.

"The man who seeks too much comfort will melt into porridge," he said.

"I could stand to be porridge for a while," I said.

***

We pretty much spent the winter indoors. There was time to talk. Turns out, Bill was an educated man. He said many of the mountain men are well-taught. Some were religious. The problem with those religious boys is that they forbid alcohol and shut down bordellos in frontier towns. Not popular, but they carry the power of the Lord on their shoulders so they can swing their weight and make significant changes.

He taught me some sign language. Straight forward, he said, the motions basically enact the words: a cupped hand toward the mouth = eat, a hand moved away from the mouth = speaking, a hand on the chest = heart, a flat hand out to one side = good, same with a fist = bad, rub back of hand = Sioux or Lacota, neck slice = Black Foot, trace an imaginary hat brim = White Man.

"Most Indians are friendly," he said. "They were astonished to see white men when they first arrived, and until the Spaniards started attacking them they were welcoming and wanted to share their knowledge. But there are some exceptions to friendly. The Black Foot are very territorial. They will trade with the Canadians because they are not taking game from their lands but they will kill mountain men on sight because they believe that the game on their land belongs to them alone."

"I always thought I'd die with a Texas Ranger slug in my heart," I said. "Now, it might be a tomahawk."

"There are a lot of ways to die out here. If you're killed by an Indian they'll mutilate your body so you can't come back in the next life with a eye to see them with or a shoulder muscle to strike someone. Then, of course, we got grizzly's in the streams, cliffs to fall off, rivers to drown in, bad weather to freeze in. Take your pick."

I looked around at the fire dying in the fireplace, the books, the food, and the whisky. "This seems like this is a pretty good way to do it. What keeps you from setting up in Kansas City with things like this to surround you?"

"The mountains cast a spell on me," he said. "I came here because I had to. I couldn't stand politicians telling everyone how they should live their lives, like I'm sure they do in Kansas City. This is a wild land where you can live the way you want. I counted on the freedom out here but what I didn't count on was the magic and the grandeur. That's enough to keep me here as long as I can manage to stay alive."

"Is that why mountain men come here?" I said.

"Some have wanderlust," he said. "They just can't sit still. They're the ones who find new pathways through the mountains to the Pacific Ocean or up to Canada. When the beaver trade gets thin a lot of these guys turn up leading caravans through the mountains. Nobody knows the terrain any better."

***

There was snow off and on through the winter and sometimes blizzards. During those times the furs and pelts became really valuable. We wore long buffalo coats with the fur on the outside, as the buffalo had worn them, fox hats, and beaver gloves. Equipped in this way, and for short times, we could stay warm as toast in 40 below.

We visited the Jumano. We wintered with them a while, during the hard times. I began to wonder if I was destined to remain a mountain man or whether I might return to my wild life as a bank robber and general ne'er-do-well. As interesting as this life was up here in the mountains, somehow I couldn't quite put out of my mind the allure of Central Texas and the exhilaration of the rob and chase game which I was so good at.

I decided that whichever course I chose would determine how, and how soon, I would die.

That sorta worried me.

David Watts

CHAPTER EIGHT

In late February when winter was beginning to lose its punch, Bill up and said it was time to go to Ft. Stanton. He took the bear fur and a few others, bundled them into makeshift packs made of burlap, tied them to our backs and we rode off.

Due to the absence of saddles we had no place to carry long guns so we had packed pistols instead and hoped for the best. The ride took three days and we had just enough food to last and just enough warm clothing and furs to survive the cold nights.

Bill knew the Mescalero Apache were all around Ft. Stanton and he knew where every settlement of the Apache as well as a few other tribes was located between us and them. Our route there was circuitous. We arrived without any attacks along the way. I was surprised.

The sentry at the Fort's gate was surly and sleep deprived and arbitrary. He was not welcoming.

"What are you here for?" he asked.

"Here to trade," Bill said.

"Don't need no trade."

Bill looked at him cockeyed. "You speaking for yourself or for Colonel Davis?"

"Colonel Davis got transferred."

Bill got steamed. "Looky here," he said. "We've traveled five days to get here and we're not going back. I've come here twice a year for the last five years at least and was always welcomed as an American fur trader. I have business to do here and you are disadvantaging your fellow troops by your hostile attitude."

The sentry looked a little shaken but quickly recovered his composure. "Just testing you, hoss," he said. He stepped down from his post disappearing behind the outer wall. A minute later the gate swung open.

"Five days?" I said as we rode in.

"Remember the lesson about lying?"

"What truth did you champion this time?"

"The magnitude of the effort involved."

The new Colonel greeted us warmly and we sat down at a table with cigars and whisky. The Colonel asked about the status of Indians around the area we came from. Bill gave him an elaborate answer that went on for five minutes about each section of each tribe, where they were, what they were doing, including the rough reception we had received from the renegade gang of Cherokee.

The colonel was amazed. "Don't know how you survived," he said.

Bill looked at me. "Part of us died back there," he said.

We entered trade talks. Bill was a master. We came away with saddles for our horses, a pack mule to carry basic supplies and a new long rifle and scabbard Bill strapped to the withers. The bear pelt was a huge hit, partly because of its high quality but mostly, I think, for the story that went with it, which Bill told in grand style concluding with a spell-binding flourish about his trying to escape underwater and my shooting the bear at the very last moment.

The colonel promised to tell that story upon every possible occasion.

We stayed an extra day to rest up during which time we fed richly upon meals cooked by someone who actually knew what they were doing.

***

A day and a half after we left Ft. Stanton, clouds rose on the northern horizon. They were the kind of clouds that boiled upward to the top of the sky and turned almost yellow in the concavities formed by the roiling, frothy peak.

Bill stopped and smelled the air.

"We got two choices," he said. "We can turn back to Ft. Stanton and maybe make it before it gets really cranky or find shelter somewhere around here because this one is a dilly."

"I thought we were almost done with winter," I said.

"It's a Freak Storm," he said. "They come any time of the year they want to here in the mountains. Summer, they're not too bad. But this time of year, when you think you're almost done with winter, they can be man-killers: winds up to 100 miles per hour, heavy snow for three days or more. A storm like this is supposed to happen in December or January, but sometimes, one of these stinkers comes along when it damn well wants to."

He waited for my opinion. I had none.

"We wouldn't make it back to Stanton, anyway." he said. "We'll just have to do the best we can."

I didn't like the tone of his voice as he said, "the best we can." To me it meant a severe distrust of the decision we'd made. I knew we didn't have much to

43

work with, still in all, up against his usually stoic, courageous, willing-to-take-on-anything kind of attitude, any little flicker of doubt was monumental.

He lifted his body off his saddle, stiffening his legs in his stirrups and looked around. The horizon ahead of us to the north and to the east was the wide open plain—nothing to stop the wind. To the south were rolling hills. The west lay high mountains with peaks and cliffs. Already the clouds were massing over the northernmost peaks.

"We go west," he said, and reined his horse directly west at a canter. I followed with the pack mule in tow.

The wind picked up suddenly, shoving us from the front and a little off to the side. It felt like someone slammed a door on us. We had to lean directly into its thrust to keep from being blown silly on our rides.

The push of the wind penetrated the small gaps around my beaver hat and curled down my neck and shoulders under my clothing. I could feel my cheeks go red. My hands stung with a hundred needles and the snow had not even arrived yet.

Twenty minutes like this and my whole body began to chill at its core, the usual small flame in my chest, shrinking and flickering in the dark.

Then the snow came. . .

. . . a few large flakes at first, quickly followed by flurries of tiny crystals spinning and swirling around us, eventually funneling into a steady stream of solid fields of snow blasting right at us.

There was ice on my eyebrows, my ear tips. Even my hands, now doing their best in beaver mitts, began to throb. Mucous from my nose froze in a long icicle.

Then came the white-out.

Vision shrunk. Objects dissolved. The mountains disappeared and we had to trudge forth hoping we were keeping our direction true. It got so bad I was riding a headless horse. Only the mane and neck could I see slipping into a featureless, smoke-like cloud of raging snow.

I suddenly had the feeling that I was isolated from the entire world, lying unseen out there somewhere around us, not even sure, at times, where Bill was, appearing and disappearing to my right or left. We were like two trout pushing against the roar of a waterfall.

I worried that our lack of visibility would lead us to the edge of a canyon or drop us into a raging stream. We could come right up against the trunk of a giant pine and not even see it coming. Yet we had no choice but to continue, danger where we stood, danger everywhere around us. Danger also stumbling into the path of a falling tree. Yet standing still was to invite a quick death from freezing into a block of ice.

Moving forward at least had the narrow possibility of shelter.

CHAPTER NINE

Time went fuzzy. I'd no idea how long we'd been at this or what time of day it was. The light couldn't tell us anything, fractured and splintered by seething flakes of snow, sliced by millions of tiny razorblades into a raging, smoky fog.

Time would pass or stand still and it didn't matter, because we were of solitary purpose, all other choices eliminated, trudging forward as if the imaginary trail ahead was a tiny thread to wedge us through the storm.

As the world collapsed around us, my life also shriveled down to the size of the small circle of vision surrounding me. Bill's cottage, Ft. Stanton, the Indian settlements, even my escapades with Banks and Trains were so far removed from me that they'd become part of a foreign continent, not even part of my own history.

Nothing, more than this small circle of air.

I suppose someone watching from some distant place, perhaps through the eye of a crystal ball, could tell how long we traveled this way. But to the two us, trapped in this moving cage made of storm, minutes and centuries came together in the same place.

Then my horse suddenly ran into Bill's and stopped. I moved alongside him and saw we were up against a wall of rock. He shouted over the roaring noise of wind to say, "Let's move along the face and see if there is an overhang or concavity we can move into."

We stumbled along the vertical cliff, our arms stretched out to feel the face of the wall to our side, guiding us. At times the wall jutted out and we had to turn away, losing sight of it until we rolled back against it once again. At times it opened into a deep crack no wider than the torso of a man, not large enough to allow shelter.

The ground under our feet became uneven, the horses stumbling at times trying to maintain footings. Just when we were about to turn back the other direction the wall opened into a deep overhang.

"Is it safe?" I asked.

"Nowhere is safe," he responded and turned into the concavity and dismounted.

Our eyes slowly accustomed. I expected to see a bear in the corner, or a giant rattler.

The walls were sheer. The floor, packed dirt. The entrance was only partly filled with snow letting enough light through so we could see a little deeper into the haze. We rested there, two horses, a mule, and two bedraggled men with mounds of snow on their shoulders, watching the storm wall up at the mouth of our cave.

We ate jerky and hardtack. Scooped handfuls of snow to make water in our mouths. We fed our animals what feed we had, saving half for tomorrow. We had enough food for the three days that we anticipated we'd need to get home. Already we'd used almost two. Bill said these storms usually don't last very long. We could hope for that. We curled up against a wall and slept.

***

Next morning the storm was still raging. Snow had piled up at our gate and tumbled into the room, stopping at Bill's feet where he lay sleeping.

"Hum," said Bill.

"What?"

He rubbed the back of his neck, working out a crick from sleeping catawampus. "Bigger than I thought. Must be a mass of cold air moving down from Canada. Something down south must have pulled it down on top of us."

"How long?"

He looked at me then out our window to a snowy world, the wind still howling. "Until it stops," he said.

***

Three days in that cave and still the snow was still five buckets down. Our cave entrance was almost covered over completely and our food supply was gone. My stomach was heavy as a rock and my body, slow as a turtle. Bill and I had started eating our belts. We had nothing for our animals but the dung on the floor.

On the fifth day Bill sliced the neck of the mule, not deep enough to kill him, just enough to get a little nourishment from his blood. I refrained. Bill said, "These are the acts that separate mountain men who will survive from the ones who will not."

I still refused.

The rocks in my stomach pinned me to the ground.

On the sixth day everything went quiet. The wind died down and birdsong could be heard through the remaining crack of sunlight at the top of our snowpile out front. We started digging through.

By noon we had a wide trench to the outer world and we lead our horses and mule into a brilliant blue sky spotted by puffs of bleach white clouds. It felt like springtime had pushed in overnight, the deep snow on the ground a harsh reminder of winter's fury.

It took two days plus a lot of hunting, and lots of stops to let our animals leaf graze off low lying branches before we finally, hungry and exhausted, dragged ourselves home.

CHAPTER TEN

I rose from my palette on the floor the following morning to find Bill's bed empty. I thought it especially curious that after such a strenuous and body-depriving spell that preceded this bright and shiny morning that he would not be sleeping until some cosmic absence within his body was filled, even if that took till deep into next week.

Not so. He was gone.

I rose, washed my face in the basin by the door, ate a little Hardtac with jerky on it and stretched my body to get rid of all the stiffness and toxins still lingering from the previous ordeal. I noticed that several books had been removed from the shelves and were strewn about on the floor. The Bible was not among those remaining.

I put on my boots, buffalo coat and fox hat and went outdoors.

It was a brilliant morning. The sky was radiant blue and the mountain peaks that surrounded us were capped with new snow that gave them both luster and sparkle. I'd seen trees weighted down with snow in pictures in a book. You could still see parts of the branches in those trees. The only part of these trees still visible was their shape. They were so full of snow they looked like they were made entirely of ice cream. White snow on the ground, white mountains. Looked like somebody had dropped a million gallons of whitewash everywhere. Only the shadows and the deeper tone of sky had a darker shade to show. I took a deep breath of very sweet air and was thankful to still be among the breathing.

The garden was invisible under a foot and a half of snow and our freshly trodden path of return was the only evidence of human activity in an otherwise blanketed terrain.

I walked out into the sunshine as if I were asking its warmth to penetrate my coat and hat and loosen up my screw-tight body. I shivered but kept on walking along the trail of hoofprints strung across the valley floor.

Maybe a hundred yards down from the cabin, footprints veered off to the side and punched into the newfallen snow a trail of departure. With my eyes I followed its path until it lead me to a person, it was Bill, sitting on a rock at the top of a medium sized hill within the basin we lived in, not as nearly as high as the surrounding peaks.

What was he up to?

Not wanting to disturb his private stroll out to this promontory of isolation I turned back to the house and restored the banked fire to blazes.

Not long after, Bill came strolling in.

I looked at him with questioning eyes. He didn't wait for the asking.

"Did you notice?" he said.

"Notice what."

"Our survival back there was not just hard work, not just good fortune to have supplies and animals of burden, and not good luck." He had been unwrapping himself from his garments and paying attention to their neat placement. He turned and fixed my eyes in his. "It's a crazy world we live in. Much is given. . ." he tossed his hat to the side, "but much we have to fight for."

I felt like he'd exposed a new chamber of his personality.

"I didn't know you were religious," I said.

"I'm not."

"Sounds like."

"Look. I come to this part of the world that is filled with majesty and danger all around, the extremes of joy and sorrow. How could you not be aware of more than just your own sweet self?"

He paused and nodded.

"That's about a close as I come to it," he said, and started fixing breakfast.

***

After fixing a mess of grits and eggs he sat down to his large repast. I watched him eat a while. He looked hearty and full of spark.

"Bill," I said.

He looked up and stopped chewing for a brief moment.

"I want my horse back," I said.

His whole body shook in vertical miniature jumps like he was silently laughing. He tilted his head so that one eye did all the looking at me. The eyebrow shot up.

"Now yr talkin'," he said.

David Watts

CHAPTER ELEVEN

"I happen to know where those Comanche hang out," he said.

"Thought you might."

"And I've had enough time to think how we might relieve them of that horse of yours without getting caught."

"That might take a little miracle."

"Miracles are hard to come by but solid thinking and the good use of all your talents is not."

"What talents are you talking about?"

Bill looked at me like he was bothered by the question, but he got up from his unfinished breakfast nonetheless, and went to the back of the house where there were some high shelves. He stood on a little stool and brought down a medium sized box and put it on the table.

He attacked his breakfast.

The box just sat there.

"What the hell?" I said.

"See for yourself," he said and pushed the box my direction.

I went to it. The box was grey with some washed out letters on the top and frayed edges that made it look like it had been sitting on that shelf for a century or more. I dusted off the top and opened the box. Inside were three sticks. My god, they were dynamite.

"Holy shit!" I said.

"That's what I thought," he said. "And by the way. . ."

"What?"

"What you're looking at is my 'talent'."

***

Bill took his damn time finishing breakfast, as if this wasn't some sort of emergency or something, dragging it out in order to create dramatic effect. Christ! Dynamite is already dramatic effect!

At last Bill cleared the dishes and spread out a large piece of paper on the table. "I've been wanting to get even with those horseasses," he said, "ever since they put us through that death chase. This will be a little slice of heaven."

I looked at the assemblage of items on the table with astonished eyes. "I've stolen money, jewels, watches. . . never horses," I said.

He nodded and smoothed out his paper, placed the three sticks of dynamite to one side, reached in a crockery jar on the shelf behind him and brought out three stogies and a small pack of matches. I'd not seen matches out here before. Must be a rare and expensive commodity. Must be he puts a high priority on this mission, something he's willing to bring out the goods for.

He drew maps, isolated the Comanche camp, indicated the large boulders and sources of water, the location where the horses would likely be kept. There would be about twelve men in camp, maybe a few more, and the horses could number up to twenty—this guy had done the job of a bank robber's advance man.

"Indians sleep with their ears open," he said. "We can't brush a branch or snap a twig if we want to come away with our scalps."

"How are you going to separate out my horse from the rest?"

"Not going to."

I gestured puzzlement, turning up one palm and hunching my head down on my neck in a little plea for an explanation.

"We're not just after one horse." He paused to let that jiggle in my brain. "We're taking the whole bunch."

I let out a loud "Yah-Hoo!" I couldn't help myself. I slapped my knee. "Show me more," I said.

***

We started out next morning. Bill had a bag of supplies tied to his back and a bow slung over his shoulder in case he had to kill someone quietly. Five arrows rode in a sheath.

The Comanche camp was twenty miles away. Horses walk about four miles an hour, canter about eight. It's an easy one day trip. But we had to calculate the arrival time very carefully.

Getting too close in daylight risked being spotted by scouts. Waiting too late in a dark night risked losing our path, making ourselves easy targets.

Bill had it planned so that we came within five miles of the camp and stopped there to wait. It was a crescent moon so there would be a short extension of light but the moon would set about ten p.m. In darkness, and after scoping out the terrain we could ride in another three miles and wait.

We arrived without complication. Bill tested the wind direction. He was the one that would be clinching a lighted stogie in his mouth so he had to go downwind and stay there.

We found cover and waited until about one o'clock. There was just enough glow from the high-altitude starlight to make out shapes of things.

Bill tested the wind again.

He lit a stogie, hiding the match flare in cupped hands.

We were standing in a small cluster of trees, the wind just strong enough to rustle the branches. Bill abruptly went stock still, cocking his head to one side. He held out his hand toward me as if stopping traffic in a cattle chute.

Slowly, gently, he slipped the bow off his shoulder and anchored an arrow in the bowstring. He seemed to be watching something.

We stayed this way, motionless for a couple of minutes.

Suddenly there was a rustle of branches and something whizzed by my head and crashed into the tree behind me.

Bill drew back the bowstring and let fly.

There was the thud of the arrow hiding something and then the crash of a falling body into the snag of dead branches on the ground.

Bill went forward and lit a match over the body of a Comanche brave. Behind us we found a tomahawk stuck in the tree.

He doused the match and then went off to his right, down wind.

I went to the left making a wide circle around camp. We both were to stay our distance until the action took place.

It took about thirty minutes for each of us to arrive at our destination, careful not to make a disturbance along the way. I knew that when he arrived to his first destination he was taking his lighted stogie and pressing it against a second stogie. He was close enough that he couldn't afford the light flash of a match strike.

When the second stogie was lit he placed both in his mouth. He then took a stick of dynamite out of his pack, secured a fuse and placed the stick and fuse on the ground. He rammed the end of fuse into the butt end of the stogie and left it there, the smoldering fire maybe an inch and a half away from the fuse tip, clearing a little space around it to keep the fire from spreading. By the time the stogie burned down to the fuse tip and ignited he would be yards and yards away.

Then he walked his horse ninety degrees around the broad circle and set another stick of dynamite in the same manner to its ignition system with the remaining stogie.

Now, not reeking of burning tobacco any more, it was safe for him to complete the remaining fragment of the circle to join me upwind from camp.

My position was high enough along the rising ground leading up to the mountain range behind me that, with the aid of the high altitude glow of starlight, I could just make out the camp.

About an hour from the time of our separation Bill sauntered up, mounted his horse and stayed side-by-side with me waiting for the fireworks to begin.

It didn't take long.

The first explosion shook the ground and startled our own horses. We anticipated this and were prepared to ride out the sudden spasms. What we were counting on, of course, was the startle and swift departure of the Indian horses from the Comanche camp in a direction away from the sound of the dynamite blast, which is the location we were stationed at. If all the horses left, there would be none left for the Comanche to use in pursuit.

What a beautiful thing it was. In the dim glow of starlight, to see an ocean of horses moving toward us was a thing of grace. As they just about reached a spot even with us Bill rode into the lead position and I into the trailing position and we directed the run of horses under our control.

This must be how horse thieves do it, I thought.

As we were settling the horses into an organized pack the second stick of dynamite went off. The distance was far enough behind us to only slightly disrupt the momentum and pack mentality of horses in their nervous escape. The pack disconnected a bit but coalesced to a tight mass of horse frames bobbing and running.

We went to the Pecos River and crossed it. We went up river and crossed back over. Farther up we went into the water again and took the horses downriver, this time a considerable distance away from the original entrance. There on the western side was a slab of rock as large as an East Coast city. We drove the horses up on the slab where there would be no hoof prints to follow and down the other side toward home.

By the time we reached the Jumano camp it was almost noon. We dropped off all the horses but for my Speed Boy and a couple of horses Bill had grown really fond of. Then we returned home.

A sense of contentment spread over me. We had paid our debt to the Jumano and the Denton Mare was mine again.

CHAPTER TWELVE

The days passed like apples ripening, slow and colorful. Following Bill around was entertaining and, at times, dangerous. We had the beaver traps to tend and the ripening new garden to harvest. Of course, we spent time over at the Jumano tribe's home ground. Bill renewed his intimacy with Morning Sunshine and I renewed my cautious friendship with Moonflower.

She continued to tend to my cuts and scrapes, the unavoidable collections of a remote life in the wilderness, and provide company through the days. It was like I was being restored to full power after each of my visits with her.

She didn't stay overnight. I was lead to believe that to do so was too great a commitment if there was no marriage in sight. Well, there might be a marriage in sight. My mind was trying to accustom itself to the idea of marriage to Moonflower. There's not much in this world better than that high quality of devotion. Besides she was, as they say, gorgeous!

To marry a girl from an Indian tribe requires the permission of the chief. That part, I thought, might not be too difficult. We seemed to get along. But there was a tradition that most tribes had of expecting gifts. A custom not to be confused with "buying" the girl but rather an expression of gratitude and honor to be given the hand of a beautiful maiden. The more beautiful, the more extravagant the gifts had to be.

In Moonflower's case, she being what I considered to be among the most beautiful in the tribe, the gifts should be in the range of two horses, several beaver pelts with a couple of mink or badger or fox thrown in, along with a gun or two with ammunition. I didn't have such wealth. But we had delivered a sizeable batch of horses. Maybe that would do.

But to marry her would be turning my back on my previous life. I might *want* to do that, all right, but I might not be *able* to do so, addicted as I was, to the chase.

The longer I thought about it the more I became divided in my allegiances. Nothing would be better than a life with Moonflower. I could chance the breaking of my addiction, but would it be fair putting her in the path of a Texas Ranger showing up at my door one day?

I lived it day by day.

She would come in the late afternoons after we had gone out on hunts with the braves and come back with whatever happened to fall within our reach: antelope, fox, rabbit, squirrel. . . and finished the cleaning, the meat processing, the stretching of the hide. I would be tired from riding and processing and she would massage my sore muscles and oil my skin with fragrances from lupine, sagebrush or the spicy scent of yarrow.

Her beauty was, for lack of a better description, of a spiritual quality, manifest most exquisitely in her glistening dark brown eyes that seemed to range deeper that my sight could reach. So different from the women I met back in the saloons of Central Texas. Her eyes didn't flit. There was a welcoming sense of openness that invited me in. We didn't need language for that.

In the late evening those eyes would glisten with unshed tears and she would rise and let me hold her close. She didn't mind my hands drifting over her baby-soft body in one last goodbye for the evening.

After she left, there was a powerful ache deep inside my body that lasted well into the night.

***

Then one morning a little later, Bill tossed water on my sleeping face and said, "Time to go to The Rendezvous."

I wiped water from my face with the back of my wrist, picked a sleep from my eye and said, "What the hell is The Rendezvous?"

"Every Mountain Man should attend the Rendezvous at least once in his life. It's a gathering of men who are trappers, hunters, adventurers, story-tellers, merchants of various sorts that come together for trading, selling, getting drunk as hell and acting like idiots."

I laughed in spite of myself. "Sounds like just the right thing," I said.

A couple of hours later we were on our way.

"Where in hell are you taking me?" I asked.

"To the Rendezvous," he said.

"Smart ass," I said. "I know that. But *where* is the 'Rendezvous'?"

"Oh, up in Wyoming somewhere," he said.

"Jesus! Why didn't you tell me it would take a quarter century to get there?"

He looked at me with mischief in his eye. "'Cause. You wouldn't have come if I did."

"Sneaky son of a bitch!"

He laughed. "You should know that by now."

We rode like forever.

Around noon he stopped, lifted his nose to the air and said, "I smell antelope."

"You can't goddamn smell antelope," I said.

"Sure I can."

I came up alongside and glared at him. "Prove it," I said.

"Okay," he said. "See that clump of trees directly ahead."

"Sure."

"And that cliff on the mountainside beyond them?"

"Think I'm blind?"

He ignored my barb.

"Off to the left there is where I smell those antelope."

"You're full of shit! Now you tell me your sense of smell is directional?"

"Off to the left, right around that clump of rocks."

I cocked my head to one side. Not wanting to be fooled by such outlandish claims I remained skeptical. "This I gotta see," I said.

"Just what I was hoping," he said.

Now I felt trapped. What next?

"I want you to go over there around the left side of that clump of rocks and scare the antelope this direction. That cliff will keep them contained and the trees will hide me until they get close. As they come along I'll pick one off and we'll have dinner."

I stood my ground.

"Wazzamatter? Got cold feet?"

"It's my brain that's cold to your fucking idea. First of all. . ."

"Listen," he said. "If you spend precious time getting all intellectual on us, those antelope will drift along out of reach and we'll go hungry for dinner. Now are you going to act on the advice of a wise and experienced mountain man or stand on your 'intellectual' training—which actually has scarce place out here in the wilderness?"

I grunted. Caught in the jaws of an improbable dilemma with both choices not worth the hot air it took to explain them.

"You're farting out your ass," I said.

"Talented, aren't I?"

Realizing I had little option, I turned and fulfilled the request of an insane, cockeyed traveling partner by riding to the place he instructed. Turns out, damn it!, he was right. As soon as I rounded the mound of rocks, out sprung three antelope running top speed around the clump of trees, and out the other side.

I heard a shot and came back to see Bill standing over an antelope on the ground.

We had a great dinner that evening and a new pelt to add to our bounty.

***

Much later, *much* later, after he had glowed incessantly upon his sweet victory against all odds, I learned it wasn't his sense of smell at all. He lied. He'd seen tracks on the ground leading to the place behind the rocks, not coming back out again.

Okay. I learned a couple things by that experience. He's not a man, he's a goddamned coyote. And second, you can't believe a thing he says.

CHAPTER THIRTEEN

On the trail three days and we meet up with Forrest Joy, another mountain man. I asked how that unexpected coincidence happened. Bill and Forrest just grunted.

Forrest is from up around Silverton and full of piss and vinegar. He lives outside the town but goes in for supplies occasionally and a little dallying at the Hardwater Saloon. Apparently, he has a favorite there, Susie. To hear him talk she's second in her face and shapely attributes only to Venus de Milo. But then, as I have learned, you can't believe anything these mountain men say.

Forrest has a sheepskin jacket with fleece showing wildly around his neck and at the low hem. He has a wood pipe he keeps clutched in his teeth even when it's not lit. Several teeth are missing, and the rest are stained yellow-orange from the constant exposure to tobacco juice. He has a gravelly voice.

So when evening comes around an old tradition got started up. Mountain men, when they travel (and probably on most any other occasion) tell stories. There are no rules except to make it interesting. . . which means, it may be based upon true happenings but the trick to wining approval from an appreciative audience lies in the rich elaboration.

Forrest was just getting warmed up when we finished dinner.

***

Beating off a Griz

"I will tell you of an encounter between two trappers and a grizzly bear in September 1831," said Forrest, "while trapping somewhere along the Laramie River:"

"They had meandered the creek till they came to beaver dams, where they set their traps and turned their horses out to pasture; and were busily engaged in constructing a camp to pass the night in, when they discovered, at a short distance off, a tremendous large Grizzly Bear, rushing upon them at a furious rate."

"They immediately sprang to their rifles which were standing against a tree hard-by, one of which was single and the other double triggered; unfortunately in the hurry, the one that was accustomed to the single trigger, caught up the double triggered gun, and when the bear came upon him, not having set the trigger, he could not get his gun off; and the animal approaching within a few feet of him, he was obliged to commence beating it over the head with his gun."

"Bruin, thinking this rather rough usage, turned his attention to the man with the single triggered gun, who, in trying to set the trigger (supposing he had the double triggered gun) had fired it off, and was also obliged to fall to beating the ferocious animal with his gun; finally, it left them without doing much injury, except tearing the sleeve off one of their coats and biting him through the hand."

Bill laughed hardy and long. He sucked on his clay pipe and scratched the side of his face. "That ain't nothin'," he said. "I can outdo that."

"I knew you was a-gonna come up with somethin'," said Forrest.

"Just you watch," said Bill.

He leaned back like he was resting on a throne high above his subjects and started in.

***

Hawsmith and the Black Foot Maiden

"Back in the early days of our presence in the mountains, most of us didn't know the ways and attitudes of the Indians out here. Some were friendly and some were murderous, and if you didn't know the difference you'd be horse meat."

"Jed Hawsmith was one of those tenderfeet we used to see around here who was brave but stupid. One day he set out with his rifle to look for dinner riding on an old pony called half-wit because he was too ignorant to cross a river with a forest fire burning at his tail."

"Hawsmith was none too bright hisself and he kinda wandered accidentally into a camp of Blackfoot Indians, the most treacherous kind. They wanted to know right away what his intensions were, since if he was there to trade they might be interested. If he was there to capture game off their land, he was going to lose his head in the most uncomfortable of manners."

"Now Hawsmith didn't know how to talk Blackfoot and he was none to sharp on sign language neither. Somehow in a strenuous and cumbersome conversation that was steeped with confusion, Hawsmith made a sign that he thought meant peace and lovingkindness but turns out to mean the calling card of the Menacing God of Coyote Revenge."

"Never heard of that one," said Forrest.

"Shush," said Bill. "Just keep your ears open and your trap shut!"

Forrest chuckled and sighed with the sharp pleasure of being smashingly told off.

Bill continued.

"The Menacing God of Coyote Revenge," Bill said, "is one of those gods who take no prisoners. He rises out of the mistreatment of his kin, the coyote, and cuts off the genitals of those who give his clan any trouble."

"Ouch," said Forrest and laughed out loud. "Ooo-wee! That's one bitch of a god!"

"Just you wait," said Bill. "Now, as you may know, the Indians are always giving the coyote trouble. They believe that he is a trickster and will lead them to harm and mayhem, so they both respect him for his cleverness and distrust him at the vary highest level. Without knowing details, you can bet that someone in that clan of Blackfoot had done a coyote wrong, had mocked him as he tried to catch a jackrabbit, had tossed stones at him when he wandered too close to camp, maybe they spit at the coyote when he was making an attempt to woo a misses."

"Now the Indians didn't think Hawsmith *was* a god himself because any self-respecting god would come on the back of a tornado or a flood, something to make an immediate impression on folk. But the god could send an emissary with a hand signal that carried with it all the power and resources of the divine, yet he might look like nothing of the sort.

And that, my friend, was a fucker you didn't want to mess with."

"You see, since they knew the coyote was a trickster. How like a trickster to send a stupid man on a dumb horse with a hand signal that meant sudden death."

"Well, they invited him in. They offered him a teepee. They fed him and he became part of the operations of the tribe. He didn't do shit but since he was an emissary of the gods, that didn't matter none."

"As time went on he developed a hankering for the chief's daughter, Windsong, and started hanging out around her, offering her silly figurines he'd carved out of oak wood. She was a little confused by his antics and puzzled by his strange gifts but, what are you going to do if a god's emissary is paying attention to you?"

"As time went on she developed a small fascination for him. Maybe it was because he was strange being white, an outsider, something mysterious. Women sometimes go for mysterious men even though they might be worthless or dangerous. Maybe underneath that stupid exterior she thought there might be something wildly surprising, something powerful, maybe. But, you see, his inability to speak the language hid his true idiocy long enough to let him slip into her affections."

"Well, turns out, the chief had his limits, even with the gods. And when Hawsmith managed with great difficulty to announce his intentions to wed the sweet young thing, the chief blew his top. He decided he would do a little test. His thought was that if this was truly an emissary of a god he would be able to get out of the worst confinement imaginable. So he tied up Hawsmith, sat him onto a bed of red aunts, and set down a teepee around him."

Forrest grunted. Bill raised an eyebrow.

"Now, I don't know what the red ants thought, but for some reason, maybe that he was far too stupid to sting, they stayed away from him. Or, maybe he just smelled bad. Whatever it was, that speck of good fortune allowed Windsong to sneak into the teepee with a knife in the middle of the night wearing her extra thick moccasins and cut his leather bindings."

"So they ran away together on foot, Windsong and Hawsmith, and reached the river just as the pursuit that had formed behind them was about to catch up. They jumped into a canoe and started paddling downstream. The Indians followed closely behind."

"Just as they were about to be overtaken, Hawsmith took the righthand fork in the river. Windsong shrieked and clutched Hawsmith in a death embrace. He just thought it was a sudden outburst of affection that he'd earned by his courage and critical intelligence. He was wrong about that on both counts. In case someone maybe didn't get the first one, there was yet another signal to the importance of that turn. The Indians in pursuit stopped on the spot and turned around."

"What Hawsmith didn't know was that the river on that side of the fork lead directly into a waterfall eighty feet high, plummeting down among rocks and the debris of fallen trees in a maelstrom of tumult and torrent. No one ever got near that death-making hazard."

Bill paused for dramatic effect. Nobody spoke.

"Now you may think that they went over that waterfall. And that is probably true. And you may think that to survive such a fall they would indeed have had to have been within the keep of the Menacing God of Coyote Revenge. And you may think that they died. And that is also probably true. I can tell you for sure that's what the Blackfoot thought."

"But, I can tell you something that might puzzle and scramble your brains, and that's that occasionally, years later, a half-breed comes down from the mountain now and then and when he gets soused enough, tells the tale of his parents, Hawsmith and Windsong, that verysame tale I just told you, like it really happened just that way."

David Watts

CHAPTER FOURTEEN

Three days later we were dead center Colorado on our way to the Rendezvous in Utah and we run into Rickles Johnstone going to the same place. I don't know if these "coincidences" are indeed just that, or due to the fact that there is a funneling effect upon a stream of humanity converging upon a celebration that makes it more likely that we'd run into old mountain men friends. In any case, here we are, facing Rickles like it was all planned.

I glared at Bill. He shot a glance that said, if you ask that question you will get the answer you deserve.

I didn't ask.

Rickles was dressed all in khakis and a straw hat. He wore a jacket made of mohair and boots with elaborate carvings along the side. He had a large belt buckle that had a map of the state of Nebraska on it and if he'd had a sprig of sourgrass clamped between his teeth I'd think he was straight off the farm.

Rickles was over from the far side of the mountain having immigrated there from the flatlands and he looked about a hundred years old though he was only thirty-five. He specialized in fox and was bringing to the Rendezvous various arrangements of fox pelts from hats to leggings to coats.

Rickles was put to the task later after dinner to provide the evening entertainment.

He settled in to tell his story.

***

White Man Who Scalps Himself

"Some visitors, up from St. Louis and friends of Bent and St. Vrain, were at the fort, among them a man known as B. Dodd. Now Dodd was as bald as a billiard ball, and mostly he wore a wig when he went out."

"One day there were a number of Indians hanging around in the fort and Dodd decided he would have a little fun with them. For some time he walked around, eyeing each Indian with a fierce and maniacal stare. Now the Indians considered most white men to be bit tetched, but this man looked like he had definitely fallen off his horse one too many times."

"Without warning, Dodd dashed into midst of the Indians, and letting out a blood curdling shriek, tore off his wig and threw it down at the feet of the stunned Indians. The Indians fled the fort like scared jackrabbits, convinced that Dodd had ripped off his own scalp."

"Even after the joke had been explained, none of the Indians could be induced to come near Dodd, referring to him as the White-Man-Who-Scalps-Himself."

***

Everyone nodded. A half-hearted clapping followed.

Directly, Bill poked the fire with a stick and said, "I feel like a story is a-commin' along and I just might have to tell it."

Forrest was quiet. So I couldn't tell if he was unimpressed or was showing some kind of mountain courtesy for Rickles. But I, for one, was glad to hear that Bill might be on for a yarn.

Seeing no objection around the fire—probably would have proceeded anyway—he commenced to tell his story. I knew he'd be making it up as he went along.

"Let's see if we can take that situation you just talked about, Rickles, and stretch it out into something a little bigger," he said.

***

Dodd's Comeuppance

"So that guy Dodd you talked about was feeling pretty cocky having fooled a bunch of Indians who had never seen a wig before. And he went into a bar with the idea of getting rightly soused in a high and celebratory mood."

"Now there was a whore in that bar who's name was Martha Ford. She had a secret past she wasn't telling anyone about. And she'd heard that story about what Dodd had done, fooling all those Indians like that. And while the rest of the people in the bar were laughing, including all the other whores, she wasn't. She just sat in the corner and made herself a little plan."

"She watched him all evening, pouring down drink, laughing, slapping his comrades on the back and telling jokes. From time to time she would saddle up to him and rub against his thigh. Being a little drunk, he wasn't sure if he actually felt her against him or if it was the wind that sometimes whistles through a bar when someone opens a door. Anyway, it made him feel a certain, really strange way."

"Well she wasn't to be denied. After a while and after a large number of drinks, she stood next to him, facing him, long enough for him not to mistake her for the wind or an apparition of some kind, and then pressed her breasts against his arm. That, he recognized."

"She walked away from him then. Whores know how to turn a man on a spit. They've seen the underbelly, the secrets of the body and mind where they come together to make the crazy and fragile parts of a person's soul. She was working his soul. And she knew how."

"Well, it was all clicking into place, her little plan. He couldn't take his eyes off her. He watched as another man paid her fee and took her upstairs. It made him jealous. He reached in his pocket to see if he had enough left to buy her for the night. He did not. He returned to his drink and drank way too fast and way too much."

"By the time Martha came downstairs again she had changed into a dress that looked to Dodd like spun moonlight. It was white as snow and her succulent form pressed against it from the inside traced her exactly, like the shape of a silk worm you can see against its cocoon. Every fold and valley of her heavenly form was visible to his astonished eyes. Yet all he could afford to do was to look longingly at her with moony eyes."

"She saw his look and recognized it for what it was. She came to him and whispered in his ear. 'I see you looking at me and I know what it means. I can see your sadness, your longing to be loved, your helpless attraction to my beauty. I know what you suffer.'"

"'Oh, beautiful woman,' he said. 'I only wish I were worthy of your gifts, only wish I could afford the pleasure of your company and your graces. I am indeed a sorrowful man.'"

Rickles interrupted. "Well, I guess he got his comeuppance."

"Hold your horses," said Bill. "Not close to being done with this one."

Rickles laughed. "Then spin on, my friend, this yarn of your strange and virile imagination."

"Martha had him where she wanted him but there was a lot more to her plan. She wandered up to him and this time pressed the mossy residence of hidden pleasures between her legs against his knee and said, "You could never afford me, B. Dodd. But in that you are celebrating this great victory of yours I will offer myself to you free of charge if you only come upstairs with me right now."

"Well, Dodd was shocked beyond words and counting his blessings in this moment of undeserved reward. He stumbled off his stool and practically fell to the floor in his drunken state of disarray. But she supported him and ushered him up the stairs, launching him into bed fully clothed."

"She lay down on top of him, also fully clothed, and pressed hard against him. She wiggled her bottom and slid up and down a little."

"'Oh, darlin,' Dodd said, 'I would do anything for you.' She just nodded and reached for a glass of whisky she had laced with Peyote and asked him to drink it down. He did so without even so much as the raise of an eyebrow. Three seconds after he swallowed the last drop he collapsed into a deep, nightmare-filled stupor."

"His wig was displaced from its usual location atop his bald pate. She picked it up and turned it over and over in her hands. She thought it was an ugly looking, disgusting thing. She took a pair of scissors and cut out a patch of hair and with it, the under-cloth that supports it right in the center of the wig. Then she turned it around backwards, took out a needle and thread and sewed it to his scalp so that it looked tilted off to one side, the missing part exposing his pate like a scalped white man. He was so drunk and so snatched into the underworld of devilish dreams he didn't even flinch."

"Then she stood for a while and admired her handiwork. She nodded and then bent over his stupor and whispered in his ear, 'My grandmother, when she was still alive, was a member of that tribe of Indians you humiliated today. May you now share in the disgrace and the mockery you forced upon them.'"

"Then she slipped out the door into the night, knowing he would feel too foolish and too much bamboozled to ever reveal how he came to be permanently wearing his shame in the form of a cockeyed, rumpled, scalped and stitched wig."

Applause.

CHAPTER FIFTEEN

Next day we were in Northern Colorado. The Rocky Mountains lined up in a row to our west. Chapin, Chiquita and Epsilon standing tall and proud and very white with the rich winter's snow lasting deep into the spring. Off to our right out east there were flat high plains as far as one could see.

The rivers were running high with snowmelt and the forests were a deep shade of green. There was an aroma of pine wafting down from the high country on the descending breezes.

Along the way the trail made its way through some aspens and oaks. The evergreens extended the lush greening up the slopes toward the high peaks. We wove and dodged as we made our way through the thick forest.

We could hear the Mourning Dove wail. I also heard a Whisky Jack, as they call it, or grey jay sing its "whisper song." I always knew the dove song but I wouldn't have known the grey jay song except for the fact that Bill told me what it was.

There's a style of riding along that is almost like dreaming: the rocking motion of the horse, the breeze sifting through your hair, patches of sunlight opening up between the branches. One can get relaxed, especially if there is no apparent danger lurking around.

Such a time opens the mind to reflection, a perspective upon one's own life that stands separately from the thread of living it. I guess we were lost in that kind of reverie, for sure I was. The world around was more like a large fish bowl, brightly lit and colored.

That's how it seemed until one moment in which there was a sudden change of tempo. I saw a flash of grey descending from a giant oak off to the right, racing across my field of vision directly ahead of me, knocking Bill completely off his horse.

In a moment like that you don't immediately appreciate what happened, or most especially, the harsh implications of it. I was stunned. It happened so fast it was not to be believed and my sluggish consciousness had to convince itself that this was something apart from the idyllic realm in which we'd been travelling.

I reached for my rifle, loaded the breech and fired. Only then did I fully understand what was happening in this fracture of time that had penetrated our peaceful ride.

A very large mountain lion turned and snarled at me. There was a blood spot on his flank where I'd shot him. There was a brief instant when his eyes lit up with rage and aggression that it looked like it would spring at me or perhaps tackle my horse. Possibly because the lion was suffering a wound it chose to slip through the forest and disappear.

Poor Bill was down on one knee, blood rushing from the side of his head, oozing between the fingers of his hand pressed against a sizeable wound.

I dismounted and rushed to find a very large gash starting at the top of his head and curling down to his ear, which was all but severed completely off his head, dangling there like a leaf ready to drop.

He pushed us away and pulled on his belt taking lose his Possibilities Bag.

"Empty it." he said.

Inside was a piece of soap, a mouth harp, some thread spun onto spools and a wooden stick shaped like a cigar. He gestured to the stick and I picked it up.

"Open it," he said.

I did. Inside was an assortment of sewing needles, one quite large. I looked up at him, still bleeding profusely.

"Sew me up," he said.

"I can't sew you up," I said. "I've never sewed anything."

"Pick up the biggest needle, thread it with the largest thread and start sewing."

My hands trembled as I took out the large needle, selected the black thread because it was thickest and struggled to still my trembling hand so I could thread the string into the eye of the needle. Forrest grabbed hold of the needle and took it from my hand. In thirty seconds he had it threaded but then he handed it back to me.

"Maybe Forrest should do it," I said.

"I want you to."

I looked at his wound. A whole piece of scalp was separated from the skull underneath where I could see white islands of bone surrounded by rivers of blood. I took my hand and plastered the scalp piece back on the skull. Starting at the far end of the tear near the top of his head, I stuck the needle into the skin. It scratched against his skull and made a rasping sound. I shivered.

"Keep going," he said.

I turned the needle under and pointed it to the other side of the wound like a canoe crossing a stream. I stuck it in several times but running parallel like that, it wouldn't come out the top.

Finally I picked up the flap of skin opposite with two fingers and angled the needle upward to meet the underside of the far bank and pushed it through to the top.

Seeing that the end of the thread was far away I pulled through a long length before tying a knot. Now, a little ways away from the top of the rent, I could pinch the two edges of slashed skin together and penetrate both of them through the tented portion with one thrust of the needle. That's the way I sewed the rest of the eight inch slash back together.

I tied the last stitch.

The ear still hung like low lying fruit.

"Sew the ear back on," he said.

"I can't. There's nothing to sew it to."

"Find something then."

I looked around for something to sew it to and was happy to notice that the closure of the long rent in his scalp had slowed the bleeding. Now to find a sewing point.

There was nothing.

Here's the situation. The ear hole was standing there, open and without cover. There was a question mark of bloody tissue where the ear used to be attached but nothing projected out far enough to sew to.

"Just do it," Bill said. "I don't care if it lives or dies but stick it on anyway."

So, I just sewed it to the side of his head, as close as I could to the place it used to be, hoping that the line of bleeding tissue would reconnect in some way to the severed ear, now turning a deep, dusky shade of grey.

Surgery done. Mess cleaned up as best we could. We rested for the night.

CHAPTER SIXTEEN

Two days later we're making camp and a rider comes up. Bill and he seemed to know each other.

It was Belzy Charles, travelling as we were to the Rendezvous. This man was decked out in a multicolored coat, a patchwork of every piece of linen he had probably ever come across in his entire life, stitched together over deerskin which showed at the collar and ruffle along the bottom. His pants were woolcloth, dyed a deep orange. He wore buckskin boots, decorated with careful carvings that someone spent hours around the fire putting in place. His hat was also buckskin and the wide brim made it look like he was about to take off the ground flapping wings out the side of his head. I could tell this man was much about image.

"What the hell happened to you, Bill Crutchton?"

Bill got up from a blanket near the fire and looked to see this new addition to our roving party. He smiled. "Me and a mountain lion tangled a bit," he said. "I think the lion got the worst of it."

Belzy laughed. "I've seen you in a lot of crazy circumstances," he said, "but never with a black ear."

"I'm okay," Bill said, "just a little jarred."

"Jarred?" said Belzy, "more like dismembered."

Bill chuckled. "Sit your ass down, Belzy. We were about to start stories."

I interceded but Bill said it would take his mind off his new ear.

Naturally, Belzy had stories, and naturally, he had one at the ready.

This is his story.

***

Walker's Plunge

"Back in 1833, when ol' Joe Walker was leading a brigade out to do some trapping and exploring for Captain Bonneville, out California way, they were traveling along the Humboldt River in what would someday become Nevada.

Now the Humboldt River is typical of a lot of western rivers, in most places and seasons a man could jump across the river. At one encampment, the river was particularly wide and appeared to have some depth. But the river water at this location wasn't clear, and being kind of milky, it wasn't entirely apparent how deep it was. Bill Craig, one of the mountain men in the party decides it's time for a bath. This is his tale as related to Thomas Beall."

"The waters of the Humbolt river are of a milky cast, not clear, so one afternoon while camped on the said stream and being the first to strip, I started for the swimming hole and was just about to plunge in when I got a hunch that things were not as they should be and I had better investigate before taking a dive. I did so and found the water was about a foot and a half deep and the mud four, this condition being in the eddy. So I waded to where there was a current and found the water a little more than waist deep, no mud and good smooth bottom. In looking towards the camp I espied Joe Walker coming and he was jumping like a buck deer, and when he arrived at the brink he says to me: 'How is it?' 'Joe,' I replied 'it is just splendid.'"

"With that he plunged head-first into that four and a half feet of blue mud.

Fearing trouble and not being interested in the subsequent proceedings, I made myself scarce by hiding in the brush on the opposite side and in so doing I ran into some rose brier bushes and scratched myself some, but I was so full of laughter I did not mind that. I peeped through the bushes just in time to see him extricate himself from the mud. He then washed the mud off as well as he could, returned to the tepee, put on his clothes, shot his rifle off, cleaned it, then reloaded it and hollered at me and said: 'Now show yourself and I'll drop a piece of lead into you,' which I failed to do as I did not want to be encumbered with any extra weight especially at that time. I was compelled to remain in hiding nearly the whole afternoon."

"Before sundown I was told to come into camp and get my supper and leave, that I could not travel any further with that party."

"I was very glad of the permit for it was rather monotonous out there in the brush with nothing but a blanket around me and nobody to talk to and my pipe in camp. I soon dressed myself and then it was time to chew. Our company was divided into messes and each mess was provided with a dressed buffalo hide. It was spread on the ground and the grub placed upon it. When supper was announced we sat down."

"I sat opposite to Walker and in looking at him I discovered some of that blue mud of the Humbolt on each side of his nose and just below his eyelids and I could not help laughing. He addressed me in an abrupt manner and said: 'What the hell are you laughing at.' I told him that gentlemen generally washed before eating. With that the others observed the mud and they too roared with laughter in which Walker joined, but he threatened if ever I played another such trick on him he would kill me as sure as my name was Craig."

"This place on the Humbolt river was ever afterward called by us mountain men, 'Walker's Plunge,' or 'Hole.'"

***

Bill rolled to one side with a pleasing look on his face. I confess, that I, too, had that sort of light-hearted feeling, having heard an authentic and humorous account of what I'd come to know of the mountain man personality, a little humor, a bunch of insanity, on top of a generally amazing ability to survive in the wild. It made me a little proud to be associated with this bunch.

Then an unexpected thing happened. Bill turned to me and said, "Your turn, Bass. You can take my place in response. Besides, it's time for us to hear something from you, anyway."

I was shocked and taken completely off guard. I hadn't anticipated telling any stories. I had no stories that came from experiences in the mountains save those I had shared with Bill. I could tell the story of the death chase to the beaver den or the one about the grizzly encounter in the Pecos Tributary but Bill had lived through those experiences, too, and I knew without asking, he'd want something new. The adventures we shared together would be his stories to tell someday.

I searched my brain but came up empty.

"All I got is stories of my outlawing back in Texas," I said. "That's not much about mountain men."

Bill leaned his head to one side, picked something from his teeth, examined it and flipped it to the side. "What makes you think we'd not be interested in your escapades as an outlaw in Texas. We all got a little of that somewhere in our blood, doncha know?"

I took another survey through my brain matter and seeing as how everybody was waiting, I just started rambling on about some of my happenings.

***

Robin Hood on a Fast Horse

"I always regarded myself as pretty inept and I never thought of robbing banks and trains as anything more than just an amusing diversion. It was like a sport for me but I also didn't like the fact that I was poor and the rich were sorry sonsabitches that cheated and stole from everybody they could."

"I dabbled in race horses a bit before I got into outlawing, and I got me a fleet mount known as the Denton Mare. I raced that mare and won almost every race I got in. That whole business of racing horses played out after a bit so I took her to San Antonio and drove a herd of Longhorns up above Dodge City where we sold the cattle to some enterprising ranchers. We each ended up with $8,000 dollars."

"We squandered all that money right fast, gambling and carousing, and we hadn't even paid for the damn cattle yet. So me and a few buddies who had no other source of income and were kinda hollow in the belly started robbing stages around the area. Trouble is, we always seemed to miss getting any really big hauls that were substantial enough to set us right."

"One day we got wind of a money train traveling from a bank in San Francisco to New York so we held up that puppy right around Big Springs, Nebraska. I made the Station Master send a false signal to the engineer to slow the train so we could ride alongside and get on. We got $60,000 in freshly minted gold coins out of that haul plus about $1300 in watches and jewelry."

"People were pretty steamed about that so we knew we had to get scarce. You should have seen how fast a whole flock of people descended on the site including the Pinkerton boys out of Chicago, and started nosing around for clues where to find us. We split up and went separate directions. I disguised myself as a farmer and started making my way back to Texas."

"I didn't quite get there."

I paused and acted like I wasn't going to continue.

"Don't stop there," said Belzy, "or I'll crack your noggin."

I just looked at Belzy with sleepy eyes. "I ran into a posse," I said, "that was looking for those train robbers that took down that money train at Big Springs. They asked me a lot of questions. I told them I was a farmer headed back to my plot around

Dallas but I'd be pleased to join their effort in capturing those nasty bandits. They agreed. They even deputized me."

"So there I was, a deputy, engaged with catching myself and putting myself in jail. But I acted the part and I followed them as they rode all over the cotton pickin' place. Seemed to me they didn't know what the hell they were doing. Lucky for me, they had no idea what the bandits looked like seeing as how posters carrying sketches of our facial likenesses had not yet reached their eyes. I actually tried to be helpful by telling them what a train robber I once knew would do when he was on the run—hide out in a haystack in some backyard somewhere."

"I never met a train robber in my life. I made up that cockamamie story just to occupy their time and keep them from thinking too much about who I might be."

"They actually looked for me in a whole bunch of haystacks. Can you believe that? I had to contain myself laughing, watching them squirts probing haystacks all over Oklahoma."

"After a while I felt my welcome was wearing thin, and since they weren't finding no one in any of those haystacks, and my false identity was running even thinner, in the middle of the night I snuck out, saddled up my mare, and lit out for Dallas."

"I hid the money in a place no one will ever find it and I kinda fell back into robbing trains and stages. Don't know why, exactly. I guess some people are born to be doctors or lawmen, or clergy maybe. I must have been born to be a bandit 'cause I couldn't quite stay away from it."

"Spent a lot of time disappearing from one spot in Texas and showing up somewhere else, using those backroads and trails that probably only me and a few left-over Indians ever knew about. And as I wandered all over the state robbing and running, I wondered what happened to that posse that I was part of for a while. Truth is, I don't know to this day whether they figured out that the hayseed farmer that lead them to turnover half the haystacks of western Oklahoma was the very same desperado they were looking for."

"Sure as shootin' they never found what they were looking for under any of those haystacks. I wonder if they're still looking."

CHAPTER SEVENTEEN

Next morning we closed off the last leg of our trip to the Annual Rendezvous, this time, held in Riverton, Wyoming. Bill—we called him Black Ear now—explained that it was a celebration of survival for another year in the wilds of the Rocky Mountains and an opportunity to sell furs and stock up on supplies. What I saw when we got there made me believe that Bill left out the most vibrant part.

Whiskey. Women. Indians who'd come to trade. It was an amalgamation of everything you might imagine. In the center of the encampment were small trading posts where men would trade for furs, buy sugar and flour, acquire a new warm jacket for the coming winter. . . all kinds of trading going on. There was a lot of whooping and hollering and some of the men were shooting their rifles into the air.

Somebody was playing a banjo and singing. A few Indians came around to offer their furs for guns, or horses, or tin cups to use around the fireside. Whiskey was high on their list and many a drunk Indian, not to mention White Men, could be seen staggering around.

As soon as Belzy caught sight of the activities he jumped off his horse and went running into the center of the action, his multi-colored coat flapping in the breeze behind him. He looked like a patchwork tent caught in a sudden gust of wind.

He must have found folks he knew for he started pounding one or another on the back, grabbing one guy in a headlock and tumbling to the ground. Both came up laughing and Belzy immediately started guzzling whiskey from a crockery jar.

Bill, Forrest, Rickles and I took a more careful entrance into the festivities stopping at various booths asking prices for sugar, coffee, blankets, and tin works fashioned as candleholders with flint and firestarters locked into the base.

Trappers from all over the west had come to get resupplied for the coming season. Convenience and money seemed to be at the heart of this whole idea. The large fur companies had come in with loads of supplies to sell or trade for the furs they would send out east or all the way to England to make beaver hats or coats made of fox or mink. Looked like to me that the big fur companies made most of the money. But there was sure enough commerce circulating around for celebration, and a natural result of such a gathering was that everyone should be in high order.

Forrest right away headed off to the edge of the celebration grounds. Around the perimeter of the Rendezvous was a circle of teepees. I saw Forrest poke his head in one of these, shift his body weight a few times as if engaged in conversation, then disappear behind the folds of the flap.

I was curious. So I went up to another of these teepees where there was a young woman sitting in the opening of tent knitting a scarf. I asked her what she was selling. She smiled and looked at me like I was a young boy. I know that look. And I know that I always kinda look that way, like a teen ager and all, skin and bones, ooggelly-eyed. But this was the first time in a long while that I felt like some one was peering into my past, into my childhood with play teepees of my own, lemonade on summer days, a scent of springtime still in the air.

She touched my hand. "Come let me show you," she said.

A Navaho blanket was stretched out on the tent floor and a few pillows were scattered around. She bade me sit beside her, which I did. She smelled of lantana and maybe a breeze off the prairie. "What is your name?" she said.

"Sam," I said.

"Is that Samuel?"

"If you like."

"I do. I do like Samuel."

She took a brush and drew it slowly through her hair. Her hair was shiny and the color of a robin's breast, long and swirly and it dropped over her shoulders in ringlets that seemed alive as they bounced and jostled with each motion she made. Her skin was milk white and her eyes were deep green. There was a freckle on her left cheek that lifted and dropped with each smile.

"My name is Fiona," she said.

By this time I had forgotten why I'd come to her door in the first place, why I had asked any questions, if, in fact, I did. Even my recent trip up from New Mexico was disappearing in my mind.

"You wanted to know what I offer?" she said.

I nodded. I felt stupid, but what else could I do?

She reached a hand to her blouse and spread the space between two buttons. "Men usually wait hours to see the flash of my skin between buttons," she said.

She spread the space wider and I couldn't help but gawk. She even unbuttoned one. She was not wearing undergarments. I could see the gentle undercurve of her breast.

I think I may have drooled.

She said something about money.
I opened my pouch.
She took off her clothes.

***

Outside, Bill was buying a new rifle. He told me about it later. He also told me that these peripheral establishments, these teepees at the edge of the Rendezvous, had been brought there by the whores who flocked to such a large collection of lusty men ready to spend every dollar they had on drunkenness and pleasure, but you had to be careful, he said, not to catch the Calamity. It was a beggar's feast and along with it came the transfer of large sums of money.

There was horse racing (betting, of course), wrestling, shooting competitions, story telling around the bonfire, tomahawk throwing. I watched one man start a bonfire with a Burning Glass, a round, clear magnifier he used to focus the sun's rays on some fluffed up cedar bark and kindle a fire. So much going on, and the atmosphere was totally unrestrained. The men must have had a lot of pent up emotions because every day they got wilder and drunker.

I emerged from my heavenly cloud in the teepee into the bright sunshine in time to see a whole line of Crow Indians arriving to the northwest, bringing furs, jewelry, weavings and pottery for trade.

There was a law against trading whiskey to Indians because of the devastating effect it had upon their culture but it happened anyway and some of the Indians got so drunk they had to be carried away.

I stumbled into the light adjusting my eyes to the glare and almost tripped over a game of poker taking place on a blanket spread out on the ground. The cards were in hand, the money in a pile in the center and, it turns out, Forrest was the man with the largest pile.

As I stepped back, I noticed Bill arriving behind Forrest and whispering in his ear. After the next hand, which Forrest folded and therefore lost both his ante and his bet, he got up and said his thanks to all concerned. As we walked away Bill told me that some men got really angry when they lose, so when winning, and before you wipe out your opponent completely, it is good to lose a hand, cash in, and come back another day.

I only saw Rickles once. He was haggling with a group of Indians over a buffalo overcoat big enough to swallow him up. I never saw him after that. My guess, he got what he wanted but had to pay a stiff price, so he just picked up and skedaddled on back home.

People seemed to know Bill so it was not uncommon that someone would stop him and ask about his misadventure. The nickname, Black Ear, caught on. It was Black Ear this, and Black Ear that. Bill took it good-naturedly.

Gambling went on all over the place and many a trapper lost what they had. On the other hand, if a person kept their wits about them they could make a lot of money. Those were the fellows who celebrated lightly, negotiated heavily, and gambled little. The most valuable commodities being exchanged were coffee, sugar, whiskey, and sex. There were a lot of ways to go home rich and a lot of ways to go home destitute.

I was surprised to see tea from China pressed into a cake, silver necklaces from Germany, glass beads—very popular among the Indians—from Italy, and wool blankets from England. Clearly, the overseas products had found ways to make it even to this remote avenue of commerce.

Medical attention was available to mountain men at the Medicine Hut and I walked by when a guy was getting a large abscess on his butt drained. Of course, medical help was not available when the mountain men were out on their own in the wilds. So the trappers got their bad teeth pulled, their imbedded splinters removed, their reading glasses changed or adjusted. They bought potions and oils from the medical men and leaves and poultices from the Indians. Bill had them look at his sewing job. They said the many blood vessels of the scalp probably saved him losing that patch of skin completely. They weren't so sure about the ear. Anyway, they left the thread in place for another week since the skin wasn't fully knit.

The days went by like stampeding horses. They began to blur and dissolve into each other. I don't know how many days we were there or how many hours I spent in the spiritual realm of Fiona's tent, but I realized that I didn't need candle holders, coffee, blankets, or belts made from the hide of cattle. What I was wanting most of all, without knowing it until now, was the companionship of a woman.

Rendezvous was scheduled to last about two weeks but the longer it went on the more angry and mean it became with those men who felt cheated or abused turning violent. Fights broke out each day and one of those caused Belzy to lose one of his most important front teeth.

A couple of people got stabbed.

That's when we turned around and headed back home.

CHAPTER EIGHTEEN

The trip back to New Mexico was long and tiresome. In the sense that we were not attacked by Indians, did not get caught up in a rainstorm or its aftermath of flash flooding, the trip was uneventful. But something had gone missing from Bill. I think the lion attack took the spark out of him, at least for a while.

I spent my time thinking mostly of what my life had offered till now. And while my years were occupied with the daring and the dangerous, even with crazy stupid things that catered to an inexplicable wildness in my spirit, there was a certain lack of satisfaction with what all that had produced.

Increasingly my thoughts were penetrated by Fiona, by her aroma which I swear I could recall to memory with just a single thought, and most of all how she knew exactly what to do that filled my need.

As we traveled south, my thoughts of Fiona began to meld with those of Moonflower. Fiona had awakened certain senses in me, mostly the gentleness of touch that in a significant way, reflected back on the times that Moonflower brought her leaves and poultices to my swollen and sorrowful feet after we had run away from our Comanche attackers.

I almost thought the images of the two women interchanged back and forth in my brain, or perhaps faded into each other. They stuck with me and like a wild horse that needed breaking, they snapped me into a calmer version of myself.

I knew Bill would surely go soon to the Jumano and spend some time with his wife. His damaged spirit would be lifted there.

Maybe it was time I should marry Moonflower.

***

Two weeks later we arrived at Bill's cabin, spent three days setting things in order, then journeyed over to the Jumano. Soon as we got there I sent Bill to ask the chief for the hand of Moonflower.

As I sat waiting for his return I imagined myself melding into this civilization of peaceful Indians. I imagined using my ability to make my way through woods to hunt and fish, to be useful to the community. And, as thinking this way brought up, to my family. That was the first time I ever thought about having a family.

It was taking a long time. Did he have to negotiate? Was the chief in a bad mood? These little vignettes that I had imagined made me insecure about how this was going. Some nervousness set in.

Bill came back after what seemed like a really long time. He had droopy shoulders. I anticipated the worst. It was worse than I thought.

He told me the news. "The chief said you take too long. He said, 'I gave Moonflower to Quick Deer. They are two together now'."

I stayed five more days. Each day I felt more separated from the life I had made there, the life I might have continued, the life, for a moment, I thought I wanted. I watched the Indians do what Indians do and I was not part of it. It landed on me what I had to do. I decided there was no sense weeping about things that come to an end.

And on the sixth day, I struck out for Texas.

POSTSCRIPT

Okay. I'm back in Texas, tearing up the countryside like I used to, robbing and running, leaving a trail of empty bank accounts with my name on the withdrawal ledger.

Me and my buddies just robbed this bank in Salado. It was easy. But the security guard had buddies of his own, who, when they heard the shots, came out of their stores and barns to add to the chase. One guy even left the barber's chair with soap suds all over his face.

My buddies and I are experienced in this situation. We split. But the pursuit was close enough that they saw us ride out. I had my fast horse and I was making distance between myself and the angry mob behind me when I passed this little girl in a tree along side the road.

I stopped and I told her that I was a mean bank robber and she better get home or she might get hurt cause there was shooting going on. She didn't budge so I helped her down and set her on her way.

All that convincing took a little while and by the time I got back on my horse a bullet struck my belt and a piece of it lodged somewhere in my back.

I rode like no tomorrow and I made it to this here meadow where I had to lay my body down, losing blood, unable to go any farther.

I think I'm going to die soon. Sure, I've come close before. But it always seemed like Death wasn't ready for me quite yet. Funny, but I don't have that feeling any more. He's changed his mind about me, Death has. I can tell.

The reason I've been telling you this big long story about me and the mountain man is because since I'm back in this robbery business I'm not going to come out the other end. So I thought I better tell you this story so somebody knows about it. Mostly, I just wanted to make sure the mountain man didn't get overlooked. Or forgotten.

Remember him for me, won't you. I don't think anybody' gonna remember *my* life: bank robber, ne'er do well, man who can't sit still long enough to be kind to a beautiful and deserving woman. . . my life subtracts from the world. His life. . . his life was the spirit of America.

I've not equaled those adventures anywhere. The exciting and dangerous business of robbing banks and trains is no peer to the wildness of mountain living, I can tell you that. Wherever I go, in my soul of souls, I will remember the Mountain Man and the times we had together. He was some kind of buckaroo, that one.

And I hope Moonflower is doin' all right.

THE END

Notes:

1. The story of the grizzly bear encounter told by Forrest Joy in Chapter Twelve is taken from: Mountain Men and Life in the Rocky Mountain West. Located at http://www.mman.us/beatinggriz.htm and is in the public domain, as are the following.

2. And the story of the man who scalps himself told by Rickles Johnstone in Chapter Thirteen is from the same source above, found at: http://www.mman.us/scalpshimself.htm.

3. The story, Walker's Plunge, in Chapter Fourteen, as told by B. Charles, is also an authentic mountain man story to be found in Mountain Men and Life in the Rocky Mountain West located at: http://www.mman.us/walkersplunge.htm.

4. "Robin Hood on a Fast Horse" is a compilation of information that is true about the horse, the cattle drive and the robbery, obtained from the Round Rock, Texas website found at: https://www.roundrocktexas.gov/departments/planning-and-development-services/historic-preservation/historic-round-rock-collection/sam-bass/. Fictional elaborations upon the brief association Sam Bass had with the posse that was looking for him have been added.

5. The situation Bill suffers in Chapter Fifteen having his scalp and ear sewed back on, is inspired by the story of Jedediah Smith who suffered a similar condition, only in his case, it was a bear.

Printed in Great Britain
by Amazon